# SURRENDER TO YOU

## CAROLINA REBELS
### BOOK 12

LINDSAY PAIGE

# ACKNOWLEDGMENTS

Thank you, Kay Garrett, for suggesting the name Jenet! I always appreciate when names are sent my way.

One final time for this series:

The biggest thanks goes to Kristalyn Thornock and Carrie Marie. I am so grateful for the time you both take to read my books and provide feedback. This series is better because of it.

Thanks to my editor, Shannon Page for being such a pleasure to work with and polishing my stories for me.

Thank you, Robin from Wicked by Design for giving me yet another cover I adore.

Lastly, thanks to you, my dear Carolina Rebels fan. The end of the journey is here and I hope you've enjoyed every step of the way. It's bittersweet, but definitely time. Thank you for your patience and support along the way. You're the best.

Copyright © 2025 by Lindsay Paige

First edition: March 2025
Library of Congress Cataloging-in-Publication Data

Paige, Lindsay
Surrender to You (a Carolina Rebels novel) – 1st ed
ISBN: 978-1-962174-09-1

# CHAPTER 1

## CAL

"I don't know what you see in her," Collin says as we walk into his kitchen. "I don't even know why she wants to come over here with you when she looks at Julie like you two are still together, sneaking around behind our backs."

She being my girlfriend, Tori. I thought I'd give the whole relationship thing a go since everyone around me seems to be in one and quite frankly, I'm over flings. But Collin brings up a valid point. What do I see in Tori? I thought she was the perfect woman. She doesn't want kids. She doesn't mind me being on the road. She doesn't care that hockey comes before her. What more can I ask for?

"She's a regular lay," I respond to my twin brother with a shrug.

"That's it? *That's* why you're with her?" he asks, stunned. "It's about time you settle down, isn't it?"

"Isn't that what I'm doing?"

Collin raises an eyebrow at me. "Do you miss her when you're gone? Are you anxious to get back home to her?"

I shake my head easily. I barely think of her when I'm away.

"You aren't settling down, Cal; you're settling."

I don't really know what the difference is or why it matters. I like Tori. She checks off some things I'd want in a woman. She doesn't pester me, though she can be annoying. She dislikes Julie because I told her once that she was an ex of mine. But for god's sake, she's married to my brother.

The best way I can describe my relationship with her is that she's a safe choice. I know exactly what I'm getting. I don't have to worry about things getting complicated. I don't even have to worry about getting hurt and if I fuck up, I honestly couldn't care less because I don't have strong feelings for her.

Which is probably a problem.

Or should be one.

"You deserve better," Collin adds.

He would think so. Even after finding out what ended things between Julie and me, he still thinks I'm better than he is. That is so far from the truth, it's laughable. The gum on the bottom of his shoe is probably better than I am.

"I'll think about it," I promise anyway. "We should get back in there before Tori gets bitchy with Julie."

It was extremely weird and hard for me at first to have Julie around again. Seeing my brother so happy has made it easier. The…incident between Julie and me seems to be in the past for everyone but me. I would've thought finding out she wasn't actually pregnant would've helped. I thought Collin knowing would've helped. Yet nothing seems to ease the guilt for the gut reaction I had all those years ago.

The memory has always haunted me. I do my best to steer clear of anything that could remind me of that part of my past. It's not as easy when my brother marries my ex-girlfriend and he insists on still including me in his life.

The depth of my guilt goes farther than anyone knows. Hell, Julie thought I didn't care at all and hated me for the longest time because of that. I cared. As soon as I walked out on her, I regretted doing it, but at the same time, I couldn't force myself to do anything about it. At the end of the day, I still didn't want a kid and I sure as hell didn't want to be with Julie. I liked her, but not enough to want to spend my *life* with her.

Then there's the fact that I have a nephew. Don't get me wrong, I love Wyatt so much, but at the same time, it's excruciatingly hard to be around him. Another downside of having an identical twin brother, who knocked up your ex who you at one point thought was pregnant, is that you can see literally what your baby may have looked like. My chest aches every time he's around.

When Julie takes Wyatt up to bed, I decide it's time for us to leave too.

"Can I stay?" Tori asks once we return to my apartment.

I shake my head. It's no skin off her nose and she leaves after a quick kiss. Another thing I like about her.

A week or so goes by with Collin pestering me to break up with Tori every chance he gets and me wondering why I'm still with her. He's gotten into my normally clear head.

As usual, in the morning despite the cold temps, I head out for a run. I need it. Maybe I do need to let Tori go. She's just…easy. And not in a sexual way. I don't have to worry about anything with her. At the same time, Collin has a point. I don't actually care about her and she does have some jealousy toward Julie. Hopefully, my run will help clear my thoughts.

My morning runs have become my new best friend. It used to be Collin, but since he married Julie, more often than not, he's off doing his own thing. I tried to hang out with Zane and then he went off and got married, too. Assholes.

So I get up before even the roosters and jog. It's always nice and peaceful. I particularly enjoy it during the winter. The crisp, snippy air helps keep me cool, even if I heat up.

And damn if my blood doesn't run hot because I'm not the only one who runs this early.

A woman jogs a short distance ahead of me. I make sure to stay far enough back that she doesn't feel unsafe. It's an ungodly hour of the day with only street lamps to illuminate our path. The last thing I need is to terrify the hot chick. I only know she's hot because one day, I was spaced out while running, but paused at an intersection as if I needed to look both ways for cars. She actually startled me when she came up next to me. Never in all my life did I think a slight smile could nearly knock me on my ass. Yet that moment came right then and there.

Ever since I first spotted her about a year ago, like a creepy fuck, I stare and watch her every move if she's ahead of me until we split off. Her body haunts my dreams entirely too often. As does that little smirk I saw. It's a bit infuriating that a woman I don't know is dominating my life like this, especially since I have a girlfriend.

My soul seems to mourn the loss of her when we split off. What a crazy fucking thought. Like my soul exists. If it does, I likely damned it to hell with the choice I made about Julie's pregnancy scare. Even without that, it's hilarious to me that my soul would mourn losing sight of someone I barely know. How is that possible? Why is it that the only term that seems to fit is my soul? As if souls are such a thing. Even more ridiculous is the idea of soul mates. But that's where my mind goes every time I see her. It's insane.

A while later after a shower, I plop myself down on my couch. My mind is still full of thoughts about the jogger. She's such a beautiful woman, and I should know. Female hockey fans tend to throw themselves at me frequently. I've seen a lot of women—a lot of extremely hot women—but there is something about this *one* woman I can't get out of my mind. It's infuriating.

The image of her seems to be ingrained in my mind. I mean, what's so spectacular about long brown hair? At least I'm assuming so since her ponytail has some length on it as it sways side-to-side as she runs. That day we happened to stop next to each other, her perfect blue eyes were like a stormy ocean. Her irises ranged from dark blue, light blue, and slivers of white. I've never been so mesmerized by eyes before. I just… if there is such a thing as a perfect look or body, she'd have it. For me at least. I didn't even think I had a type until I saw her.

Like I said, it's annoying how much I want a woman I don't know. It's frustrating how much I think about her. It's stupid given how I could probably approach her, but for some reason, I haven't.

All of a sudden fingers snap in front of my face. I blink and see my brother. I have no idea where he came from, but obviously he's here for a visit.

"What the hell is going on with you?"

"Nothing," I answer. "What do you want?"

He cocks his head a bit. "Why are you grouchy? It's a beautiful Saturday morning."

"I'm fine."

Collin eyes me skeptically as he takes a seat next to me. "Sure you are."

"Why are you here?" I repeat.

"You've been extra crabby lately. Just wanted to check on you. Wait a second." Collin angles toward me. "Have you finally broken up with Tori? Is this about a new girl? Are you crabby over a real, live, decent human girl? Please say you are."

I roll my eyes at his excitement, but my lack of a verbal answer spurs him forward.

"Holy shit. There *is* a girl!"

I stand and walk away. Only to lean on the recliner so it puts some distance between us. "There is no girl." Which is true. There can't be a girl when I've never spoken to her. And again, I'm still with Tori for what little that's worth.

"There so is. Who is she?"

"Don't you need to be with your wife?" I snap, which only fuels him.

"Oh, she must be a tough nugget to crack if you're acting like this. What did she do? Completely ignore you? Tell you off?"

"I've never even talked to her," I admit with a defeated sigh.

Collin's brows shoot up. "Why not? Who is she?"

"Just some girl I see on my runs." The urge to grimace at calling her *some girl* is hard to ignore, but I keep my features even.

"Well, why don't you talk to her?"

"I'm still with Tori," I remind him.

My answer shouldn't surprise him, but his disappointment is evident.

"About that…" His voice trails off only for a moment. "Julie is ready to beg you to break up with her. I guess Tori made some comments again last time you guys came over and she's over it. Like over it to the point that she's not welcome back at the house ever and Julie refuses to subject herself to spend any additional time around her."

"What kind of comments?"

"Like how Wyatt looks so much like you."

I stare at my brother for a moment. *Of course* his son looks like me. *I* look like Collin. That tends to happen when you're half of an identical set.

"She thinks Wyatt is *mine*?" I ask incredulously when it clicks.

Collin simply raises an eyebrow at me because it wouldn't be the first outrageous insinuation Tori has made. After a moment, he continues as if I never interrupted him. "Julie's even willing to set you up on a blind date with one of her friends. Apparently, you two are perfect for each other."

I stare at him for a moment. "You want me to break things off with my girlfriend to go on a blind date that *Julie* set up?"

Collin glares at me for my implication. "You and Julie are on good terms. Even if you two weren't, she wouldn't fuck over one of her friends. So, break up with Tori. Go on the blind date. Get my wife off my back. It's as simple as that."

"What do you know about her?" I ask out of curiosity. Maybe going on a date with someone new will rid me of my thoughts about the jogger. And it'll force me to break up with Tori. I honestly don't care either way if she stays or goes, but I'm not a cheater and it's clear my brother and Julie are over Tori's bullshit allegations when it comes to Julie and me still having a thing for one another.

"Julie says she's pretty, super nice, but doesn't get out nearly enough. She wouldn't tell me too much because she'd rather you learn about her on the date. Even if you don't, please break up with Tori. It's a huge red flag that you don't give a damn for her; all you're doing at the very least is wasting her time—time she could be using to find someone else."

I sigh, knowing he has a point. "Fine. Tell Julie to set it up."

Collin grins like a cat who caught the canary. I take a seat in the recliner while he goes on about what a relief it is that I'm breaking up with Tori. I don't understand why he or Julie care about my relationships. I mean, I know my brother loves me and wants me to be happy, but since marrying Julie, he seems extra hard up on me finding a happily ever after. Julie too, oddly enough. I've stayed with Tori because I don't think something like that will ever happen.

Hockey is the love of my life. It's all I'll ever have, even when I'm not playing anymore. There's never been a plan B. There's never been a plan post-retirement. Everything revolves around the game and remaining by my brother's side.

While Collin talks, I pull my phone out of my pocket. Breaking up over text isn't the nicest thing to do, but again, I don't really care. It only takes a moment for Tori to respond to my text that we've run our course and we're done.

TORI

Just like that? That's it?

CAL

That's it.

TORI

Suit yourself.

See? Ideal woman. She doesn't even care that we're breaking up. Sure, that should probably be a red flag that she doesn't care and neither do I, but emotions aren't always the best thing to have. That's one reason why I haven't approached the woman I see on my runs.

She'd make me feel a hell of a lot, I bet. Something tells me she'd force me to face things I'd rather forget, things that scare me. And if there's one thing we should all understand about myself after all the events in my life, it's that I'm a coward.

# CHAPTER 2
## JENET

I watch as my ex, Jasper, tickles Caroline, my daughter. He went from a young, immature man who joined the Marines after high school, later finding out I was pregnant, and strutting around with his high-and-tight haircut to maturing and taking care of our daughter as best he can.

He's stationed at Camp Lejeune and for the most part, the weekends are the only time he can see Caroline. He drives the roughly two hours to his mom's house—where I'm currently staying—and has Caroline for the weekends he can come home. Sometimes my parents get annoyed with me for always freely giving her up when Jasper comes home, but considering how often he can see her and how often he may go in between visits, I certainly am not going to keep our child from him. It also doesn't help that when I had to move out of my apartment because they tripled the rent, I moved in with his parents.

My own family didn't want to take us in because apparently I'm too grown to be living with them again. Having a child and falling on hard times wasn't a reason to come back. So, I gratefully accepted the offer from Jasper's parents. It's been harder than I thought it would be to find a place to live;

I'm almost to a point of buying a house. How crazy is it that right now buying would be cheaper than renting?

Caroline finally wiggles free and makes a run for the kitchen, where her grandparents are. Jasper looks to me and whistles.

"Hot date?"

"Blind date," I correct.

His brows furrow. "What are you talking about?"

"Julie, the girl I met at the library? She set me up with someone. She has been pestering me for forever, so I figured it was time to give in when she brought it up yesterday."

"What do you know about him? Where are you meeting?"

"Not much," I admit. "It's her brother-in-law. I'm running late, though. I'll text you when I get there."

"Have fun," he calls after me.

Honestly, I don't know why I'm doing this other than Julie is sweet and begged me. I met her and her son, Wyatt, at the library during story time for the kids and we hit it off. While there's an age difference between our kids, we still get together for playdates and such. Even after all these months of knowing her, I question now if I know enough to go on a blind date. She's a pretty private person. But a date sounds nice.

Maybe it'll get my mind off the guy who runs behind me. He's been running behind me for just over a year now and never says a word. Never tries to catch up and chat. Even when we manage to stall at an intersection at the same time, he doesn't say much. One would think I would take that as a sign he's not interested, but the way he looks at me when he is close enough? It's only a glance, but damn. That look haunts my dreams. That look says *everything*. It makes me think all sorts of dirty things. If only his mouth would do some talking too.

With a sigh, I push the man out of my thoughts and walk up to the pub-style restaurant Julie directed me to. She wanted something casual and light. Cal, the name of the man I'm meeting, is supposed to be waiting outside for me. All I know to look for is a man wearing a white beanie.

I stop short when I see the man who carefully follows behind me every morning. My heart gallops when I see he wears the hat. Nervously, I tug on the white scarf I was told to wear. Oh boy. The man, Cal—I finally know his name—scans the area and lands on me. He stalks toward me immediately. Can someone's gaze truly smolder? His does, I swear.

"It's you," I breathe as he closes the distance between us.

"Jenet Brown?"

I nod. Cal graces me with the most beautiful smile and holds his elbow out for me. To say I'm speechless is an understatement. I don't even know what to focus on. The fact is that Cal is even hotter in a pair of jeans, plain navy long-sleeved shirt, and his white beanie, something I didn't think was possible. His five o'clock shadow makes me shift my weight to rub my thighs together. I can only imagine how that feels.

Or maybe the fact that the man I've been lusting after all these months is who Julie picked to go on a blind date with me. Or the simple fact I'm about to spend some time with the guy who's taken over my thoughts for far too long.

We're quickly seated and our drink orders are taken.

"Did Julie give you as many details about this as she did me?" he asks.

"She just said you were her brother-in-law."

"She told my brother you were pretty, nice, and needed to get out more." When I frown over that comment, he quickly adds, "I'm sure she didn't mean anything by it." Instead of letting me respond, he changes the subject. "So, how old are you?"

"Twenty-three. You?"

"Twenty-seven. Ever been here before?"

I shake my head. Cal comments he hasn't either and we take a moment to look over the menu. After we place our orders, I can't help but ask, "Why haven't you ever talked to me?"

I would've never thought the man could look shy, or maybe embarrassed, but his cheeks turn a faint pink.

"I didn't realize you wanted me to. I also didn't want to scare you or be creepy somehow."

I raise an eyebrow at him. "And running behind me all this time isn't creepy?"

He laughs a little. "I can't help it if we share part of our routes. I kept what I thought was a respectable distance. And until recently, I also had a girlfriend."

I'm not entirely sure what to say to that, so I change the subject. "What do you do for work?"

He tilts his head ever so slightly. "You don't know?"

"Why would I know?"

"Julie never talked about what her husband does? How long have you known her?"

The way he asks makes me straighten in my seat. It's like he's accusing me of something, but I don't know what or why.

"A couple of months. Julie doesn't talk much about her husband's job; we have other things we chat about."

He studies me for a moment before saying, "We're hockey players. We play for the Rebels."

Jasper will lose his mind! He's a huge sports fan and is currently making Caroline that way too. I don't even watch a lot of TV. But I do know the names of the pro teams in our state and I know the Rebels is one of them.

Cal pauses and then adds, "Her husband is my twin."

My brows shoot up. "Identical twins?" He nods. "There are *two* of *you*?" I ask more to myself, wondering how the world revolves like normal when there is another human out there who looks like Cal. "Wow," I absentmindedly breathe. I don't know if I could even be in the same room as them both without literally swooning. Pushing the thought away as Cal chuckles, I ask, "What's it like having a twin? Or even being a pro athlete?"

Cal leans back in his chair. "It's just like having any other pain in the ass sibling, but worse because we're too often on the same page, I guess. Playing hockey is great. It's what I've always dreamed of and sacrificed so many things for." I swear his face loses color.

"Wait," I say, just now realizing what he said a moment ago. "How recently did you become single?"

"Like two days ago. Why?"

I frown. "Julie's been trying to set me up for months."

For some reason, Cal laughs. "She didn't like my girl-friend, so, not surprised." He pauses as our food is delivered.

Maybe I'm a glutton for punishment, but I find myself asking, "Why didn't Julie like your girlfriend?"

Cal doesn't seem all that surprised or bothered by my question. "Guessing since Julie wasn't that forthcoming, she didn't mention I dated her in high school?" My brows shoot up at this. "Long time ago and as you know, she's married to my brother now. Tori, my now ex-girlfriend, didn't like knowing I dated Julie so she kept accusing us of things."

"Oh wow. Things like that certainly aren't fun to deal with."

"You have experience?" Cal asks with a touch of skepticism.

"Well, I have a five-year-old, I have a good relationship with her father, and I live with my ex's parents. Dating isn't exactly easy sometimes for either of us."

Cal stares at me for the longest time. For so long, I squirm in my seat. The waitress drops off our drinks and still, he stares at me.

"Excuse me for a second," he says, his chair scraping loudly against the floor. He rushes away, his phone already to his ear.

When five minutes pass, I sigh heavily.

Well.

I guess that's a deal breaker. He's probably calling Julie right now to ask why she set him up with a single mom. That has to be it, right? Why else would he act so weird? What a disappointment! I've waited so long to talk to him and now I wish I never had. My daydreams and fantasies were better than real life. Figures.

With a sigh, I grab my purse from the back of the chair and begin the walk of shame out the front door. Okay, so maybe that's a bit dramatic, but my kid-free night has been wholly unproductive.

"Jenet, wait!" I hear once I'm outside, about five feet from the door.

Reluctantly, I turn to face Cal. "Look, it's fine. You'd clearly rather watch me run from afar than go on an actual date with me. It's not the first time I've sent someone running and it won't be the last, I'm sure."

Cal exhales heavily. "Will you please come back inside with me?" He rocks on his heels and I'm surprised he seems nervous. "I'd say I'm not normally an ass, but I probably am."

"Is that supposed to make me want to go with you?" I question incredulously.

He chuckles and his small grin nearly steals my breath away. "Please?" he asks, holding his hand out for me to take. When I don't answer right away, his hand lowers ever so slightly. "I'm not used to this."

"Dating?" I ask, confused further when he nods. "Didn't you say you recently had a girlfriend?"

Cal sighs. "Yeah, but," he winces, "I didn't put any effort into that. Please come back inside with me. I've waited a long time to meet you and I promise I won't be such an ass."

"Every other thing that comes out of your mouth makes me think I should head on home." I finally take his hand. My heart flutters at the contact and his barely audible sigh of relief. "I want it noted that I'm ignoring red flags to come back inside with you."

Cal grins brilliantly. "Noted."

Before I can change my mind, Cal turns and pulls me inside. It's clear he's concerned I may get up and walk out because when we return to our booth, he ushers me into my seat and then slides in next to me.

"Blocking my exit?"

"If that's the way you want to look at it."

The waitress tops off our drinks and Cal angles toward me a little. "Before I so rudely interrupted, you mentioned an ex and a kid?"

"Yeah, my ex-husband and my daughter."

Cal's brows rise. "You were married?"

"And divorced," I confirm. "What a list of accomplishments at twenty-three, huh?"

"More than I can say for myself personally. My last girlfriend was my first since college. And she was a real winner considering Julie and my brother had been begging me to break it off with her for nearly the entire time I was seeing her. Sounds like you're doing just fine." When I can only stare at him for a moment, he laughs and says, "Seeing another red flag?"

"Seeing lots of them. I think I liked it better when you didn't talk."

"Noted."

He falls silent and we continue to eat. It starts to feel awkward, so of course I fill the silence.

"I got pregnant right out of high school. Jasper had already enlisted with the Marines, but when he found out, he swore he would do what he could to help take care of Caroline, our daughter."

Cal seems to still and tense next to me, but he remains silent. I can't help but ramble forward.

"We got married, eventually got divorced because we're

better off as friends and co-parents. I moved back home to have more support nearby and after some bumps in the road, I found myself staying with his parents because mine can be assholes sometimes. I need to move out, but it's also nice to have support literally right there in the house."

Cal pokes at his food with his fork. For some reason, I feel as if he's still truly listening to me. Even as his gaze flicks back and forth between me and his food, it's startling how handsome he is.

"Why am I here still if you won't converse with me?"

He grins. My breath catches in my throat. "You said you liked it better when I didn't talk. I only meant to accommodate."

Without thinking, I slap his arm with the back of my hand. "That's just mean."

"Maybe I need to see if *you* have any red flags," he replies, amusement full in his tone. He tilts his head and pretends to think while tapping his chin with his forefinger. "You live with your former in-laws, that's a definite red flag. You get along with your ex, which would probably flag some people. And lastly, you're attracted to my brother."

"I am not!" I immediately deny, shocked he would accuse me of such a thing. When Cal laughs, his face transforms into a handsome sight, and I'm stunned for a moment. *Again.* Lord, I need to get a grip. He's just a man.

"I do believe you said and I quote, 'There are two of you? Wow.' Clearly, you are attracted to me, so you'll find him attractive as well."

I purse my lips. "I think you're poking fun at me and I'm not sure I appreciate it."

He nods, but his smile remains.

When he doesn't speak, I decide to poke back at him a little. "You know, I didn't think a pro athlete would have so much trouble talking to women."

His lips twitch. "I don't have trouble talking to women."

I smile. "I'm the special one then?"

"While you are special, I think I'm doing okay talking to you."

I perk an eyebrow, proving I disagree.

"What do you do for a living?" he asks, ignoring me.

"I'm an interior designer. I help folks decorate their homes, offices, and help relators stage houses. I love it and it gives me flexibility, which is good considering Caroline. I'd ask you about your job, but I wouldn't really know where to start. I don't know much about the game, despite Jasper's best efforts."

Cal shrugs. "That's fine. How'd you meet Julie?"

I share that I take advantage of the children's programs and events the local library offers and I met Julie and Wyatt there. Overall, Cal is quieter than I would have expected, especially now that I know he's a professional athlete. But he does keep the conversation going. He asks things like if I've always lived in North Carolina, what I like to do for fun, and about my family.

As the food disappears from our plates and the date clearly draws to an end, Cal seems lost in his own thoughts once again. I'm tempted to break the silence, but something keeps me quiet as well.

His voice is soft, his gaze too intense, as he finally speaks. "I haven't been able to get you out of my mind since I first saw you. While this blind date is likely a dud compared to what you are used to, I would appreciate a second chance. I'm not...I don't..."

Cal sighs and something twists my heart at seeing who I'm sure is a normally confident person fumble over his words.

"Red flags everywhere," I whisper, which makes him laugh. "But if you want a second date, sure. I expect to be swept off my feet, though, so the red flags can be more easily ignored."

"I'll keep that in mind."

He tosses some cash onto the table and stands, holding out a hand for me. I take it and then Cal leads me out of the building. We exchange numbers and then he sees me off, promising to talk soon.

Unsurprisingly, Jasper waits up for me. It's not late, but late enough that Caroline is already in bed. Because his parents like to act as if they're eighty, they are also.

"Well?" he prompts as I plop down next to him.

"You're not going to believe who it was."

At this, he perks up.

"Cal Kessy."

"Cal Kessy, as in Carolina Rebels Cal Kessy? Your friend is married to Collin Kessy? How did you not know this?" As an afterthought, he adds, "How did it go?"

"I don't know. It was weird. Rocky."

"He's got no game?" Jasper asks with a laugh. "Maybe he's too used to having women thrown at him that he doesn't know how to work for it."

I wouldn't say Cal has no game, but it's like I threw him off by saying I was a single mom and then everything was stilted.

"I told him I'd go on a second date."

Jasper raises an eyebrow at me in surprise.

"He's hot, Jasper. And he's also the guy I see on my runs."

"Ah, the mysterious runner. That explains it." He throws an arm around my shoulders. "Just be careful."

The funny thing is we're one dud date into this thing and I already feel swept away.

# CHAPTER 3

## CAL

I drive straight to my brother's house after parting ways with Jenet. Learning she has a kid—easily my biggest fear outside of what I will do when my career ends—caused me to call my brother and cuss him out, even though it was his wife who set it up. I should've known Julie couldn't be trusted.

"Well, how did it go?" Julie asks, practically bouncing on her feet when I barge into their kitchen. Clearly, Collin did not relay our earlier conversation. "I asked Jenet, but she hasn't texted me back yet."

"Did it ever occur to you that I don't want to date someone who has a kid?"

"Cal," Collin warns, but I ignore him.

Don't get me wrong, I'm fucking thrilled to have finally talked to the woman who crawled beneath my skin before having ever spoken a word to her. But there's also something about her that makes me want to run far, far away. Anyone can guess what that *something* is. I'm not sure how to deal with that.

I've avoided talking to Collin about this because he always seems to think I'm better than him. That I'm infallible.

Even after he learned about what happened with me and Julie, I can't be as open with him as I need to be. Now he's married to Julie. The past is the past. They have moved on; I'm supposed to do the same. Yet my decision haunts me everywhere I turn.

At work, there's Collin.

At team events, there's everyone's kids.

At games, there's the kids cheering on the team.

In public, there's the random happy dad, playing with his kid.

And I'm left to wonder *what if*.

What if I hadn't been so selfish? Yes, I know there was never a kid, but I didn't always know that. Wondering what may have happened to that unborn kid started eating me alive at some point. For years, the idea of a mini-me kid brought nightmares. Collin marrying Julie is honestly a living nightmare. There goes my life's biggest regret, staring at me in the form of my nephew.

Granted, neither of them seem as disgusted with me as I am. Well, Julie did at first. She isn't as bothered now. She's moved on. She's happy.

I'm still being tortured, though. Collin would tell me to get over it. I've been trying. *God, have I been trying*. Nothing works and I'm not sure how to do it.

And now, Julie has unwittingly forced me to face my nightmare.

"You should've told me, Julie," I tell her. "I wouldn't have gone." Though, thinking that after knowing her friend is my jogger pains my heart as I likely never would've gotten the balls to go up to her while running.

"You can't be serious," Julie states, dumbfounded for some reason. "Jenet is a great person and you are blowing her off because she has a *kid*? Have you not grown up at all, Cal?" she asks incredulously.

Her question causes me to flinch and Collin steps closer to

her. "Julie," he says quietly, already settling in to play referee between us. Toxic air now fills the room, heavy with the past.

"*No!*" she snaps much like I did earlier. "After all this time, I was starting to think you actually had a heart in there, but you're proving me wrong once again. Please don't stand there and act like you care about walking away from me when we all know you'd do it in a heartbeat all over again."

"*Fuck you!*" I explode. I'm so sick of her saying I didn't care, though over the years, it rarely came up.

Collin steps toward me, placing himself between us.

Pure agony has sat heavy in my chest every fucking day since I walked away after she told me she might be pregnant. It has covered my insides like black, gooey tar. I can't get rid of it; my very being is irreparably tarnished.

"You have *no* idea what I feel, Julie. You have no idea what it was like for me to think for *years* there was a kid walking around that looked just like Wyatt does and I. Didn't. Know. Him. Every damn time I saw *any* kid, I wondered. I *regretted*. My choice suffocated me. I made a stupid fucking decision because I was terrified of something interfering with the *one* thing I'd worked my ass off for my *entire* life.

"How dare you act like I have no heart when I've been haunted for *years* and continue to be haunted by the what ifs. And Wyatt," my voice cracks as all the steam suddenly escapes me. "I love him to death, but you don't know how hard it is to be around him."

I take a deep breath. "I have no regret walking away from *you*, but every second since then, I've regretted abandoning the baby that never even fucking existed. I imagined its life for years until you started dating Collin and I found out the truth. Some days, it's like there *was* a baby who later died and I'm stuck with the regret and horror of having never met him. I don't know how to get over that."

My chest heaves with my confession. Terror slithers through me as they stare back at me and I realize everything I just admitted. Julie's phone pings on the counter and she glances down.

"Wait, you're taking her out again?" she says after reading the message.

Collin ignores her. "Why didn't you tell me you've been carrying that around all this time?"

I bark out a laugh. "Me share with my twin who thinks I can do no wrong? Even after Julie opened your eyes by telling you what happened, you still give me the benefit of the doubt and think too highly of me."

Julie surprises me when she softly says, "I'm sorry I made this worse by not telling you sooner. But you do realize the only one still holding a grudge against you is yourself, right? It used to be the first thing I thought of when I thought of you and now? It doesn't cross my mind because I've left it in the past where it belongs, and you were there for Collin and me after what happened with Dwight. You need to let that go, Cal, or you'll never be happy."

"And how the fuck am I supposed to do that?" I ask.

Neither has an answer for me.

"Maybe you should see Trace," Collin says just when I think the weight of the silence will suffocate me. I'm not surprised in the least he thinks his therapist can help.

My gut wants to snap I'm not crazy and don't need a therapist, but that comment would hurt my brother. One good thing about Julie being around is I can see how I made my brother feel like shit for his anxiety and I work to stop making inane comments like I used to. Collin isn't crazy, I know that; there's nothing wrong with him.

"Yeah, maybe," I agree. What would it hurt?

"Why are you going on a second date if you didn't want the first one?" Julie asks.

My gaze flicks to my brother. "She's the girl from my runs."

He grins and then laughs.

"What?" Julie asks with confusion.

"He's been obsessing over her for a year because she runs ahead of him in the mornings. He can't walk away even if he wants to."

I scowl, mostly because he's right.

"She says I have red flags," I say, focusing on the next important thing, which causes both of them to laugh. "Date two is my second chance, but she said I need to sweep her off her feet." And then I do the one thing I never thought I'd do. "Julie, I need you to help me plan something since you know her better than I do."

Her eyes light up at the idea. "Absolutely." She reaches across Collin to grab my hand. "I promise you'll overcome this," she says quietly. "I harbor no ill will and considering we've all ended up where we should, anything I can do to help, I will. Maybe Jenet will help heal those wounds too."

That would be too much to ask for. While I don't necessarily want to date Jenet since she does have a child, I also can't imagine not indulging myself by spending more time with her. I feel utterly fucked and excited all at the same time.

———

I stand beneath the lamppost at the intersection where Jenet and I tend to separate and hear footsteps pounding the pavement. When Jenet gets close enough, she smiles.

"Figured there was no sense in stalking you anymore," I say, hoping she can hear the humor in my tone.

She chuckles. "So you admit to stalking to me? That's, what? Red flag number one fifteen?"

I laugh. "Come on."

We begin our run and I find myself being quiet again. Smooth-talking girls while I'm trying to get into their pants is one thing; talking to a girl I would like to continue seeing while at the same time run far away? That's a whole different story.

"So you *are* tongue-tied around girls," Jenet says with a chuckle after a few minutes of silence. "Am I that scary? Between the two of us, I should be more intimated by you. You're supposed to be some big hockey star, have loads of money, and I'm sure you have girls throwing themselves at you all the time."

I clear my throat and force myself to talk to her, as if this isn't a big deal. As if being here with her is just another day. I ask about her family again and learn that she has four sisters. Both of her parents are still alive and so are her grandparents. She's the third born. She was the first to have a kid. Learning all this about her means having to share some about myself. So, I tell her about my brother and my parents. I tell her about my rise in hockey, hoping she realizes as I explain it just how important the game is to me.

Why I care that she knows this, I don't know. I've sacrificed and caused so much damage fighting for the life I live. If she doesn't understand that this is my life, then there's no hope. When she asks me about my retirement plans, my body freezes as we reach an intersection. I have no answer. That's another thing I avoid thinking about if possible.

"You haven't thought about it? You can't play forever."

As if I don't know that.

"All I know is hockey. I'll probably go crazy when that time comes. I wish I had an answer." Especially because if something unexpected happens and knocks me out of the game before I'm ready, I'll be utterly lost.

"You have no other interests?" she asks me incredulously.

"What can I say? I'm pretty simple."

I sound lame. I can't help it that my entire life has been invested in a sport. There are times when I wonder if it's all a waste. That is such a terrifying thought. To think all I've worked so hard for has been for naught? I mean, I do have another interest that no one—not even my brother—knows, but fat chance in hell of me sharing that with anyone.

"I can't figure you out, Cal," she says.

Same.

Once again, I find myself at a loss for words, but once again, Jenet picks up the slack.

"Jasper has been talking about signing Caroline up for skate lessons. She'll play T-ball in the spring, but Jasper wants her to love being an athlete like he was, so he wants to sign her up for everything, but...I don't know. No matter the sport, I worry about her getting hurt."

My throat dries up at the mention of her daughter. "Pain isn't a bad thing, Jenet. Sports help you grow." Sometimes, in not so great ways, as in my case, but there are good things about being involved in a sport. "It might not be bad to let her learn and test different things out."

To get away from the topic of her daughter, I tell her about learning to skate. How we got started in the game. The impact it's had on my life as we make our way back to where we met up. As we slow to a stop, I can't help but look her over. Her chest heaves from exertion, her lips part with her heavy breaths, and my gaze lingers on her mouth.

"You can't kiss me until you blow me away on our second date," Jenet teases, pulling me away from my desires. "When will that be, by the way?"

I shrug as if there's no rush. "I'll let you know once it's all planned. Between my schedule and yours, we'll need to figure out when we can even go."

Jenet stares at me for a beat. "Wait, you do know I was kidding about it being extravagant, right?" When I only stare at her in reply, her eyes widen. "Cal! I was kidding. Don't waste too much of your time and money on a second date over a comment made in jest."

"Regardless, I have to make up for our first date and I'm in charge of everything this time, so I'm taking advantage. I'll text you in a bit to lock down a date; just let me know if something comes up and you need to change it. Would you be able to get away for the entire day?"

A small sigh leaves her, but I don't miss the faint smile she wears. "You're gonna go all out, aren't you?"

I only grin.

"As long as Jasper or his parents can keep Caroline, I should be able to do that. Please don't go crazy, Cal. I'm not a high-maintenance woman, I swear."

At this, I laugh a little. "I won't go overboard," I promise. There's nothing else to say yet I don't want her to go. What the fuck is wrong with me? "I won't be here tomorrow," I forewarn her. "I'll text you if that's okay?"

She nods and I release a breath.

"I should go," Jenet says as she throws a thumb over her shoulder.

She should. As should I. My feet lock into place, rooted as if her presence grounds me and until she walks away, neither can I. My gaze drops to her mouth. It's been so long since I've started watching her and now I've been in close proximity to her twice in twenty-four hours. The fact that I've yet to kiss her seems ridiculous.

"You sure I can't kiss you?"

Jenet smiles and good god *damn*. "If you have to ask…" She shakes her head and tsks. "See you soon, Cal." With that, she takes off running.

Meanwhile, I stand there feeling as if my world shifted on its axis, tilting so sharply I'm sliding and sliding, waiting until I fall into the abyss. As it's been since I first caught sight of Jenet, I'm helpless to do anything about it.

# CHAPTER 4

## JENET

A week and a half passes before I'm able to see Cal again. We've texted here and there, but nothing too crazy. But today…today we finally get our second date. The fact that Cal is picking me up at eight in the morning does nothing to settle my nerves.

Caroline frowns from where she sits on my bed.

"What's wrong?" I ask.

"You aren't spending today with me and Daddy?"

"Hey," Jasper says, walking into the room. "I thought you liked days when it's just the two of us."

"I do!" she insists. "But why can't Mommy come with us?"

My chest aches and for a moment, I wonder if I should stay. As if reading my thoughts, Jasper shakes his head at me.

"Mom has somewhere to go today, but tomorrow, we're both all yours," he promises.

That seems to satisfy her. I give her a hug and a kiss and then head outside where Cal already waits by the curb. A smile rests on his face as I slide into the passenger seat.

"Ready?" he asks.

"I'm not sure. What are we doing?"

His smile grows. "You'll see. How was your week?"

"Good. Jasper thinks it's sacrilegious that I'm dating you, or whatever this is," I stutter, "but have never been to a game."

"Do you want to do that?" he asks with a hint of nervousness. I'm unsure why, though. Is it weird for my heart to warm at how he maybe realizes I'm not a huge sports fan and he's not trying to push it on me?

"I am curious to watch you play."

The grin he gives me takes my breath away. "I'll let Julie know and she'll take you."

"Can I bring Caroline? Jasper has her interested in anything sports-related and I think she'd enjoy it."

He falters so briefly I wonder if I imagined it. "Yeah, of course. Julie will bring Wyatt, too, I'm sure."

"What are we doing here?" I ask as he turns into a nearby small airport.

"You wanted to be swept off your feet," he reminds me.

"I was kidding!" He can't be serious. "We're flying somewhere? I can't just leave. I have—"

"We're just going for today. I'll have you home tonight," he promises.

I'm stunned speechless. Dazedly, I follow Cal once he parks and soon, we're walking up the stairs onto a small plane.

"I've never flown," I admit as we buckle in.

Cal interlocks our fingers. "I do it all the time. It's a quick flight. Want me to talk and distract you?"

When I nod, Cal wastes no time. He talks about hockey almost entirely, though. He wasn't kidding when he said he was a simple man; there doesn't seem to be much more to his life than hockey. There's something about the way he talks about it—a desperation, maybe—that makes it clear he's devoted his entire life to the sport. So much so that it makes sense why he has no idea what he'll do without it.

"Have you thought about broadcasting?" I ask at one point. He would have the personality for it, I bet. Not that I watch sports, but if I can be mesmerized by him talking about the game, maybe that's the route he should go when the time comes.

"I haven't thought about anything," he admits. His thumb has been rubbing the back of my hand the entire time, but I think its has more to do with soothing him during this conversation than me for flying. "But I'll add it to my list of possibilities. Look."

He gently nudges my chin toward the window next to me. The city looms below us; it's such an awe-inspiring sight. I've never felt so huge and small in my entire life.

"Where are we?" I ask without looking away.

"New York City."

My gaze is glued to the sights until it's clear we're about to land. Cal chuckles when I close my eyes and squeeze his hand.

"You promised not to go overboard," I remind him.

"I only planned what I think you deserve. Julie helped."

I grumble under my breath, making Cal laugh again. A short bit later, we exit the plane and get into a waiting car. Already, he's spent more money on me than Jasper probably did the entire time we were married. My brain itches to protest because it's entirely too much already, but another part of me who hasn't been on a date in far too long—who hasn't had a day of fun outside of time spent with my daughter—is all too eager to soak up today.

Our first stop is a bakery Cal likes to frequent when he has time in the city. We eat breakfast and then walk around, seeing places I've only ever seen on TV. He takes me to various tourist attractions, holding my hand the entire time. We stop at a nice restaurant at some point. I feel entirely underdressed, but we're escorted into a private area and I have the most delicious meal of my life.

After lunch, he takes me on a helicopter ride to view the city from the sky once more. We get a couples massage and he throws in a facial and manicure for me as well. He takes me shopping. Despite my protests, he buys various items of clothing for me and he even buys a stuffed animal and blanket I spot after making a comment on how Caroline would love it.

As the day winds down, I'm entirely too overwhelmed by all we've done. Cal leans over as we walk out of a restaurant after eating dinner and says, "Two more things, the best yet, and then we'll fly home."

"I don't know that my feet can stand two more things," I admit.

He laughs and says, "It'll be worth it, I promise."

The car that's been carting us around all day takes us to the next destination. Christmas time in New York City is almost magical. When Cal takes me to view the tree at Rockefeller Center, I'm awestruck at the sheer size and beauty of it in person.

"Properly wooed yet?" he asks with amusement in his tone.

"Not sure," I tease, dragging my gaze from the tree to him.

"You will be. Come on."

On the car ride over to wherever we're going next, I lean against his shoulder, utterly exhausted but tickled pink on the inside.

"What time does Caroline go to bed?"

I lift my head, unsure why he's asking. "Eight."

Cal frowns. "Sorry you'll miss bedtime; that's important, right? Collin calls Wyatt when we're on the road to say goodnight, even if it's before his bedtime so they can at least say goodnight and whatever. Is she expecting you?"

"Jasper's home and I already gave him a heads-up." It's sweet he's concerned about that, though.

"This is our last stop before we go."

We've stopped outside of a tall building and Cal leads me inside and into an elevator that takes us up and up and up. And then we go further by taking a set of stairs onto a rooftop. I gasp when I see our final destination.

There's a freaking ice rink on the rooftop! Christmas lights and small trees decorate the space. Music plays loud enough to be heard, but not so loud that conversation can't take place. There's two people on the roof, seemingly waiting for us.

"I can't skate."

Cal chuckles. "I figured as much. C'mon."

Once we exchange our shoes for skates, Cal helps me onto the ice. I have no idea where to look—at the gorgeous man who can't stop smiling or at the city alit around us. Both blow me away.

"Cal, this is…" My voice trails off as I struggle to think of a word that encompasses our day and my feelings.

He easily skates backwards, pulling me around the rink. He's been so charming and happy all day. I certainly wasn't expecting him to do all of this.

He slows to a stop and pulls me flush against him. My breath softly swooshes right out of my lungs.

"Properly wooed now?"

"I thought you didn't know how to do this?" I ask, remembering his comment from our blind date.

His grin nearly blinds me. Cal rests his forehead against mine. "Turns out it's not as hard with the right motivation."

"And that would be?"

He quirks an eyebrow and I feel silly for having asked. I guess *I'm* the motivation.

"I want you to say it," he tells me quietly. One arm locks around my waist and his other hand sneaks between us until he grasps my chin and tilts my head up until our lips are a breath apart. "Tell me I've wooed you."

My body shudders as his lips touch mine when he says *woo*.

"You've thoroughly woo—"

Before I finish, his lips press hard to mine. It's unlike any kiss I've had before. As if he's making a statement with his mouth, hard and unyielding. But then he gentles, his tongue requesting entry that I readily allow. If one can make love with just their mouth, then that is exactly what Cal does to me. If it wasn't for the fact he's holding me up, I'd be melted onto the ice.

My hands hold onto his shirt, gripping it tightly as if he might step away from me. The wind whips around us, bitting at any bare skin. Yet my body is like a cozy fire, warm and relaxed. Cal seemingly explores every inch of my mouth before pulling away.

It was too perfect. Too heavenly. My eyes stay closed as if I can stretch out the moment even longer that way.

Cal chuckles. "Let's see if I can get you skating somewhat on your own before we have to go."

We spend the next forty-five minutes where he teaches me how to skate. Well, he tries. I can't quite get the hang of it, but I do manage to wobble around next to him.

Before long, we find ourselves back on the plane. Exhaustion weighs my limbs as I lean over and rest my head on Cal's shoulder.

"Thanks, Cal," I murmur.

He kisses the top of my head and I doze off. I can't believe the day we've had. It's over the top, but so much fun. I sleep on the flight back and half doze as Cal drives me home. When he parks along the curb, he takes my hand.

"There's a game tomorrow if you want to come. You can bring Caroline and Jasper and meet up with Julie and Wyatt there."

Part of me thinks I need time to recover from today, but Jasper and Caroline will be so excited about this.

"It's an early game," Cal adds. "Starts at five."

"We'll go," I agree easily.

After all the fun things we did today, now is when Cal looks like a kid in a candy store. Clearly, he loves his job and the game.

"Great." He leans over and places a hard kiss on my mouth again. "I'll get it arranged and Julie will reach out with all the details."

The porch light flashes and I laugh. "Sorry. Jasper thinks he's funnier than he actually is. Thanks for today."

"You're welcome. See you tomorrow." He gives one more kiss and then I force myself out of the car.

Jasper leans against the couch when I open the door. "Well?" he asks. "He kept you all day. How was it?"

I lean against the door and sigh. "It was wonderful. He took me to New York City. And he's arranging for us to go to a game tomorrow."

Jasper grins. "Oh, I think I'll like this guy."

I laugh, but sober with a sigh. "I feel like I'm in over my head, Jasper. Cal is…" I shake my head. "Too much," I finish. "He took me on a day trip to another city, spent god knows how much money, and even took me shopping." I hold up my shopping bags as evidence.

Jasper smiles. "He's spoiling you, Jenet. And you deserve to be spoiled." Jasper closes the distance between us and gives me a hug. "I'm happy for you and I hope things continue to go well."

Oh, so do I because so far, I love spending time with him. I just hope he doesn't think every day has to be like today. And tomorrow, I get to see him in action. See him in his element. It's clear his career means a lot to him. His job makes me a little nervous because if he gets traded and moves away, what am I supposed to do? I can't just up and take Caroline away from Jasper. But that's putting the cart before the horse and most certainly is something to worry about another day.

# CHAPTER 5

## CAL

My brother nudges my arm from where he stands next me while we stretch during warm-ups. I follow his gaze to the area I've been actively avoiding. Jasper, Jenet, Caroline, Wyatt, and Julie stand at the glass. Everyone's wearing jerseys, except for Jenet. She's wearing a T-shirt that looks too big. Is it Jasper's? Why does that put a damper on the fact she's wearing it?

"You going over there?" Collin asks.

"No." I'm being a coward again. Me skating over won't be inappropriate when it comes to Caroline, but I can't find it in myself to do it. "You go. Say hey to Wyatt and give Caroline a puck."

Collin opens his mouth, but I skate away. I catch Jenet's eye and briefly smile at her before shutting out the world to focus on the game, which is soon underway.

Out of all the years we've ever played, there's something different about this season. There's something in the air. More grit. More determination. A greater cohesiveness with the team. Scotty and Brayden have somehow upped their play, as if this season is the one in which they especially need to give their all.

Even my chemistry with Collin is off the charts. The entire team is a force to be reckoned with. Don't get me wrong; things haven't been easy. We're not invincible or undefeated; we've had some crazy winning streaks, though.

All I want to do is capture this feeling. Bottle it up and drink it every morning. This is what I live for. The breeze as I race down the ice. The roar of the crowd when we score. The influx of bodies crashing into me, coming together for a hockey hug to celebrate a goal. Hell, I even love when another player rams into me so hard, he knocks the breath out of me for a moment.

This is pure bliss. Even with the fact that our dad is the one who pushed us into the game and fed our love for it, being on the ice or surrounded by my teammates is one of the few places I've felt true happiness.

Part of me hates that fact. Every aspect of my life is wrapped up in a fucking game that will *end* one day. I'm not scared of dying. I'm not scared of ending up alone. I'm petrified of the day I lose *this*. I worry I won't be able to function. Not after everything I've done, given, and sacrificed. I *need* the game.

Even coming off a win, the black tar that covers my insides seems to sit heavier than normal. I know why. Jenet and Caroline were here. Well, still are. A big part of me wants to bail and go straight home, hoping Jenet did as well. That plan falls apart as I realize she's still here when Collin convinces me to go out and meet Jenet. He doesn't give me much of an option either. He has Julie bring her down to a waiting area. My muscles are tense, wondering if her daughter will be with her.

I worried for nothing. Caroline and Jasper are nowhere to be seen. Jenet looks anxious as her eyes bounce around the room and she nods as Julie talks, though I doubt she's really listening. What could she be nervous about?

"Jules," Collin says first, gathering their attention. She

releases Wyatt's hand and he runs over to Collin, who grins like he just won the lottery. "Hey, bud. Ready?" Collin asks Julie, who nods.

"See you guys later," Julie says, flashing the both of us a smile.

A beat after we're left alone, Jenet laughs. "That wasn't weird or anything, was it?"

I decide to ignore it entirely. "Enjoy the game?"

She smiles. "Yes. You're definitely in your element out there." She pauses and then adds, "I didn't intend to come down here, but Julie insisted. I'm sorry if I overstepped, especially since you're now my ride home."

"I don't mind. Did Caroline and Jasper enjoy themselves?"

"Yeah. Caroline was tickled by the puck."

I nod because that's good to hear. We're quiet as we walk out to my car. Once inside, I ask, "Do you want to go straight home?"

"I don't want to intrude any more than I already have; I don't know what your post-game ritual is."

See, Tori would have given me a straight answer. Not whatever that just was. I subtly take a deep breath. She's trying to be nice—I realize that—and my inner asshole wants to find something to bitch about.

"I don't mind spending more time with you if you want to hang for a bit," I reply honestly.

When I glance over at her, she flashes me a smile. "That sounds good; I don't need to hurry home yet."

"Okay with watching a movie at my place?"

She nods, so I head home.

It's been a long weekend. A good one, but busy between the day trip to New York and then the game today. I hand Jenet a remote to find a movie and change my suit out for a shirt and sweats.

I grab us bottles of water and then take a seat next to her on the couch.

"What'd you find?"

She eyes me for a moment before saying, "People always talk about *Lord of the Rings*, but I've never actually seen it. Want to watch it?"

"Sure. It's long, though. May not be able to finish it."

"That's okay."

I ask her to hop up and then I lie down on the couch. It's been a busy weekend. Might as well get comfortable. Jenet raises a brow at me, but I hold my hand out. She hesitates for a moment, but rests on top of me. I run my hands up and down her back or through her hair.

After about ten minutes of that, there's a slight shift in her breathing.

"When do you need to be home?" I ask.

"About an hour," she mumbles sleepily, confirming my suspicions that she is on the verge of falling asleep. "Your hands feel so good."

I chuckle. If I wasn't so tired and content, I'd touch her more sexually. Just a little bit. There will be time for that. For now, holding her is perfect.

This is…weird.

I've never had this. Tori and I never cuddled. I certainly didn't with my one-night stands. I absolutely love this, though. It's nice. It feels…homey. Who knew cuddling is what would do me in?

———

A couple of days pass. I text Jenet and call her some when I can, but today, I want to see her. I will tomorrow on our run, but that's too far away. Feeling out of my comfort zone, I call her.

"Hey, Cal," she answers, slightly breathless.

"Hey. Bad time?"

"No, just staging a house for a relator. What's up?"

"Want to go out for lunch?"

There's a pause, which makes me hate that I called at all. She'll say no. Maybe I misread things. This lack of confidence and certainty is a pain in my ass and I hate it.

"I'm on a bit of a deadline and need to get this done. I don't have enough time to run out, meet you, eat, and then come back," she replies apologetically.

"But you still have to eat, right? I can bring something to you if that works better."

"Yeah, I can do that," she chirps happily. "I'll text you the address. When were you thinking?"

"Now?"

Jenet laughs. "Okay, that'll be fine."

"Text me what you want too. Anything at all."

"You don't want me to choose. I stress eat and it won't be healthy."

"Don't worry about me," I tell her. "Just text exactly what you want and from where. And yes, I'm sure."

Her voice softens. "Thanks, Cal. See you soon."

We hang up and within a few minutes, she texts me her location and her meal request. Looks like she's feeling Mexican. I can accommodate that. Thirty minutes later, I pull into the address she gave me.

"You must have the wrong house," a shirtless guy says as he exits the house and spots me. "No one lives here."

"Jenet's inside, right?"

His eyes narrow, but he nods. I walk past him and into the house. Jenet stands in the living room, eyeing the current furniture arrangement.

"You know this guy?" the guy follows me inside and gets Jenet's attention with his question.

"Cal!" Her eyes light up and she walks over to me. "You guys can take your lunch and we'll finish up when you get back," she says as another shirtless guy walks into the room.

They both eye me as if I'm about to harm Jenet at any moment.

"You sure?" the new one asks. "We can stay and keep working."

She waves them off as she plucks the bag from my hand and smells the food. They hesitate. When Jenet lifts her head to see them still standing around, she frowns. "Go. Enjoy a break."

They reluctantly leave and Jenet leads me to the kitchen where we sit at a small table.

"Thanks for this. You have no idea how much I needed a break and food."

"Who were they?" I ask instead. She works with shirtless men all day? No, I don't like that. It's ridiculous because I have no real reason, but yeah, no. Not a fan.

"Oh, I'm so sorry! I was so rude. That's Owen and Greg; they are the muscle who help me move furniture in and out of the houses I stage. You really didn't have to get me what I asked for," she says as she hands me my much healthier lunch.

"I didn't mind."

She smiles. "This helps ignore the red flags. You're good at wooing and distracting me."

I laugh. "Whatever it takes."

I was starting to feel antsy, but couldn't figure out why. I'm still don't know why, but being here with Jenet relaxes me. Which makes me nervous. It's like I'm starting to need her. I'm not sure I *want* to need her. Sitting with her for thirty minutes while she explains the process of staging the house and an upcoming job where she's helping some woman redo her home is literally the highlight of my week. What the hell is happening to me?

Jenet walks me out when the guys return. I hold onto her waist and make her lean against me. A certain body part is doing more of the thinking today. It feels like it's been forever since I got laid.

"How much wooing until I get you naked?" I ask as my lips blaze a path on her neck, up her jaw, and then to her mouth.

Jenet laughs and gives me a familiar answer. "If you have to ask…" She laughs again before kissing me quickly and returning to the house.

The next time I get her alone, she's mine.

Later that night, a restless energy buzzes in my veins. It's too late to text Jenet, which means I need to expunge this energy myself. I find the hidden supplies for my secret hobby before settling in on the couch.

With the sketchpad propped on my drawn up legs, I draw the only thing I've been able to draw lately.

Jenet.

Art was my first love—as brief as it was. Dad found out about it and to say he wasn't thrilled was a massive understatement. He wanted us in hockey and art was a distraction. Art was for pussies. It didn't help that Dad could already spot the support Collin needed and how I relaxed him just by being present. Since we were always a force on the ice, his dream became our dream and I was told in no uncertain terms that art had no place in my life.

I get antsy sometimes, though. This energy bubbles and boils beneath my skin. Hockey can't even expel it. My love for drawing and painting have been a secret ever since I realized it relaxed me and Dad forbade it. My obsession is as real as it is with hockey. To the point that I rent the studio apartment next door for my use whenever I really need to get away and get lost in the paint.

Dad was so vehemently disgusted by the fact I enjoyed this creative outlet that I locked that part down. I became what he needed of me.

Someone to look after Collin.

Someone Collin could look up to as the image of strength when he felt none of his own.

Someone to play hockey with Collin.

Don't get me wrong; I love hockey and honestly can't imagine doing anything else.

But I need this too and almost just as much.

This is something that's all *mine* and I covet it like the treasure it is. Collin often thought he couldn't exist without me, but it's the other way around. At least, that's how my dad always made me feel; I have no purpose if not being support for Collin and his partner on the ice. Art is the one thing I have for and to myself entirely.

My pencil moves effortlessly over the paper. This is one part of art that I love the most. The ability to jump in, not think, and create magic. It's the similar to hockey in that regard.

The image is the same one I've been trying to perfect since I first saw it. That little smirk Jenet gave me on our run when we paused before crossing the road. I can't seem to get the image just right and it's been infuriating. Doesn't stop me from trying, though.

After a couple of hours, my body sinks into the couch as it relaxes. Finally. I can breathe easier now. I hide my supplies in the event someone shows up unexpectedly and then fall into bed.

————

"Hey, Jenet," I answer my phone over a week later. Christmas has come and gone and January is in full swing. I'm going out of my mind wanting to see her, but our schedules haven't matched up.

"Hey." Just one word, but I can already tell she's a little

nervous. "I have a favor and you can totally say no." She pauses and I just wait. Jenet sighs. "Jasper was supposed to take Caroline skating today to see if she'd be interested in lessons but apparently, he has to go into the field. She is so upset and was really looking forward to it. Would you mind showing her? Not as my…you, but as you know, *you*. Cal Kessy, hockey player extraordinaire?"

I laugh, even though nerves fill me at the idea of spending time with her daughter. The thing is I'm still pretty mesmerized with Jenet and unfortunately, I'm not sure the word *no* exists in my vocabulary with her.

"What time?"

There's a lull and and then she breathes, "You'll do it?"

"Yeah. Just tell me when."

"Oh my gosh, Cal. You have no idea how much you just saved the day. Can you meet us there in thirty minutes?"

I agree and she hangs up to get them ready. The moment the call disconnects, the heaviness of what I agreed to settles over me. Maybe I should call Collin and have him meet me there with Wyatt. Or maybe he could go in my place and pretend to be me. Jenet likely can't tell us apart yet. No, that would be ridiculous. Collin would expect better of me. With a sigh, I get ready and head to the practice facility.

We arrive within a few minutes of one another. Jenet exits the car with a grateful smile and helps Caroline out. Caroline stands behind Jenet, but pokes her head around curiously.

"Since Daddy had to work, Cal is going to show you. Remember when we went to the game and that guy gave you the puck?" Caroline nods her head. "This is that guy's brother, Cal. They both play hockey."

Caroline plays the shy card, so I wave at her and then we all walk inside. We get Caroline in a pair of skates and then I lace up myself. Jenet decides to wait on the sidelines, which shouldn't surprise me, but it hits me I'll be on the ice alone with her kid. I'm not equipped for this.

At all.

I'm sure to find a way to fuck this up for Caroline and then Jenet will walk away. I've never felt pressure like this before.

I don't like it.

Fuck.

# CHAPTER 6

## JENET

Cal seemed nervous for some reason as he led Caroline onto the ice. So much so that I nearly asked if he was okay and certain he wanted to do this. After a few minutes, it's clear he relaxes. My ovaries explode watching him with Caroline. There is just something so endearing about watching a man with a kid.

And when that man is Cal, who is concentrating on showing her the ropes and focusing on whatever she says, and that kid is my daughter?

Ovaries officially melted away.

I hesitated about asking him, but Caroline was so bummed about missing this and not seeing her dad this weekend. And it's not like I'm introducing Cal as my boyfriend. He's literally just a hockey player right now.

After about thirty minutes, it seems that maybe Caroline is ready to move on. Cal glances at me, asks Caroline something, and then when she nods, he picks her up. He skates off the ice and nods for me to follow. He walks over to another rink and places Caroline where she sits on the wall. He holds onto her waist to keep her steady.

"She's a figure skater," he explains.

Caroline is mesmerized as the girl twirls and does a jump. We watch for a few minutes before Cal picks her back up and sets her on a nearby bench to take her skates off.

"What do we say to Cal?" I prompt.

"Thank you," she tells him.

"Welcome, kid."

Once their skates are off and shoes back on, we all walk outside together. It's tempting to ask him out to the movie I have planned next. Aside from the fact I doubt Cal would want to watch a kid's movie, it's too soon to have him spend any more time with Caroline.

Caroline thanks him again and then I help get her into the car and into her seat. When I close the door and turn around, Cal stands so close to me.

"Thank you for this."

He shrugs. "You needed a skater and I happen to be the only one you know well enough to ask." His gaze drops to my mouth and I take a small step back.

"No," I warn.

He laughs. "I know. The thought is nice, though. You free Wednesday for a bit?"

"I might be able to move some things around," I tease.

His gaze does a slow sweep over my body and I suddenly wish it was Wednesday more than my next breath. This is the look that haunted me for a year while we ran. This is the look that screams how much he wants to devour me. I don't even remember the last time I was devoured. Maybe never?

"See that you do," he murmurs. And then he leans down and waves at Caroline. "Later, Jenet," he says to me before walking over to his vehicle.

I spend the rest of the day with Caroline, doing some fun things with her and getting some nice one-on-one time. I think it's time to seriously start looking for a place to live. It's been convenient and helpful to stay with Jasper's parents, but it's been long enough. I've wondered if they still feel like grandparents with us here all the time.

I message one of my realtor friends and ask for their help finding something. At some point after dinner, I get a text, but it's from Cal.

CAL

Is it Wednesday yet?

JENET

Not quite. Sounds like you're pretty anxious for it. Have big plans for us?

CAL

Big, big plans. I'll need at least four hours with you. You'll be able to make the time?

JENET

FOUR hours? What do you have planned?

CAL

Nothing I'm willing to put into a text message, but if you want to call me, I'll certainly go into all the detail you want. Just be alone if you call.

My heart hammers. Don't get me wrong; I was pretty sure before what his plans involved. But he sounds so *ready*. I don't think I've ever been with someone who was so eager to be with me. I loved Jasper and never thought twice about our intimate time together, but looking back, he was a bit selfish.

Not entirely a surprise considering our age, but it makes me wonder what kind of lover Cal will be. My body heats and my mind goes wild with all the possibilities. Will he be selfish too? Or more of a giver than a taker? Maybe an equal opportunist? Maybe he's into things I've never done before. Or am even aware of. I read. People can be pretty...kinky.

A wave of nerves wash over me. There's no doubt I'm more inexperienced than Cal. That's presuming he takes advantage of being a professional athlete and falls into whatever bed is offered to him. Am I ready to be with someone else? It's been quite a while. Almost three years. There was only one person briefly after Jasper.

My phone vibrates with a text and I hesitate to open it before curiosity gets the better of me.

CAL

Jenet? You still there? Please don't tell me I scared you off. I can plan a good four hour date instead if you want me to.

And just like that, my anxiety falls away some.

JENET

Still here. I'm good. Your plan is fine. Just make sure to feed me.

CAL

Was planning that.

We'll need the fuel.

If I wasn't in a room with my ex-in-laws, I'd fan myself. Wednesday can't get here soon enough.

———

Cal told me to wear a nice dress. My nicest dress is a navy one. The sleeves fall to my elbows, the neckline dips in a way that teases but isn't revealing, and the skirt falls just past my ankles. Perfect for this time of year.

One of my meetings ran late, which led me to getting ready late, and by the time I'm ready and it's time to go, I'm a bit frazzled. Like I need more time and there's not a chance to even breathe and relax.

"He's here, dear," Carol, Jasper's mom, says from where she stands, peering out the front window. "He can come to the door, you know."

"I think he's avoiding that since Caroline is here."

She nods, and I can tell she still doesn't like it. Oh, well.

With a deep breath, I try to steady my heartbeat, grab my purse, and walk calmly out the door. This time, Cal leans against his SUV as he waits for me. That brief moment in which I tried to calm myself is gone the moment I lay eyes on him.

Jesus, he's beautiful.

He probably wouldn't like to be called that, but I can't help it.

His khaki slacks fit him well and his shirt begs to be unbuttoned. I laugh a little, making him smile as his eyes stop their perusal and meet mine, when I realize he's wearing a navy shirt.

"We match," I explain.

"We do. You ready?"

I nod and he opens the door for me. I try to focus on my breathing as he walks around to get in himself.

"Sorry it's a bit early, but with Jasper not home, I wanted to get you home in time for Caroline's bedtime," he says.

Gah, he's too sweet.

"Thanks," I tell him sincerely. The handful of dates I've been on since my divorce from Jasper were completely different than what it's been like with Cal. None of them were considerate of the fact that I'm a single mom.

"Good week?" he asks as he takes a turn.

"Yeah. I've been hunting for a place to live. It's time. I found a little house not too far away to rent. We move in this weekend. I just need to tell Carol and Jacob."

Cal glances over at me. "You think they'll be upset?"

I shrug. "Maybe. They get unlimited access to their grand-daughter right now and that will reduce, but it's not like we'll never come over. I just feel like I'm taking advantage at this point and I want to make sure they really feel like grandparents and not live-in babysitters for me. I don't have them watch Caroline a ton, but more than my own parents."

My parents tend to find themselves busy more often than not, but that's another story.

"That's good that you'll have your own place again. You're looking forward to it, right? I can't tell."

"Yeah, I am. Have you had a good week too?"

He nods. "Been some crazy shit going on with the team lately, but we're playing well."

"What do you mean?" I ask.

He waves me off. "We can talk about it another day. For once, I don't want to talk or think about hockey." He reaches over, finds my hand, and interlocks our fingers together.

I certainly won't protest that.

A few minutes later, he pulls into the parking lot of a restaurant. My brain checks out a little once we walk inside. He made reservations. Has anyone ever made reservations for a date with me before? I don't think so.

The tables are small and intimate. The lighting low and decor romantic. Soft music plays in the background. We talk, but hell if I know what about. All my mind can focus on is how Cal keeps one hand under the table. Our knees touch and his hand runs in circles over and over on my knee. He's not even touching bare skin, but damn if it doesn't turn me on all the same. I want to squirm in my seat.

After we eat, he stands with his hand extended to me and tilts his head toward the empty dance floor. He wants to dance? The last time I danced was at my high school prom. Jasper and I didn't have a wedding ceremony. We just went to the courthouse. It was all we could afford at the time and neither of our parents were thrilled enough to spring for a wedding.

My arms wrap around his neck and his hands fall onto my

hips. Lord, he smells so good. Why do men always have to smell good? He feels nice too. Strong. Warm. Cal pulls me even closer to him until my body is fully flush against him.

Do we need to dance? There are better things we can do with our time. We only have but so much, after all. When I take a step back, Cal frowns in confusion. My heart beats rapidly and my chest rises and falls with my slightly accelerated breathing.

"Thank you for the wooing, but we can go to your apartment now."

His frown lifts into a smile. "Best thing I've heard all week. Maybe even all year."

He takes my hand, throws money on the table as we pass it, and leads me out to his vehicle. His hand rests on my thigh. How is something so simple sending me into a tailspin?

It's been too long. That's the only explanation.

Before I can fall down that rabbit hole, we've made it to his apartment. He hurries me inside, locks the door behind him, and his mouth crashes into mine.

A moan I'd probably be embarrassed about if I cared enough rises out of me.

"I've been thinking about this for way too long. Probably an unhealthy amount of time," he murmurs as we bump into walls, kissing all the way to his bedroom. But when the backs of my legs touch the bed, he pauses. "You good?"

I grab fistfuls of his shirt and yank him back to me in answer. I need him yesterday.

He hums against me, "Mmm. Eager."

He has no idea. Now that we're alone in his bedroom, a frantic energy flows through me. I reach for his buttons blindly as his mouth derails over to my neck. In the next moment, my dress is lifted over my head and he nudges me back onto the bed. I watch, mesmerized as if I've never seen such a sight before as he undresses before me.

He calls out another girl's name, confusing me for a moment before he adds, "Set an alarm for seven fifteen tonight."

Gah, even now he's thinking ahead and trying to make sure I get home at a decent time. He crawls over me and all my thoughts are consumed by this man.

# CHAPTER 7
## CAL

"I'm fucked," I tell my brother later that night.

He has the nerve to laugh at me. "Sounds like you got fucked."

"Collin, I'm serious."

It's been an hour since I dropped Jenet off and I'm wrecked. After fucking seven ways to Sunday like we were two people starved of intimacy, she unfortunately had to go home. I've been sitting on my couch, staring at a blank TV screen since. It was torture to let her leave. I've yearned over her for like a year, have gotten to know her some, and now I've had her. I feel like someone with a newfound addiction, eager for my next hit.

"Are you really that concerned over finding a woman you actually like and want to see again?" he asks.

Yeah, I am. "She's got a kid."

That fact bears repeating. She has a kid! A cute kid who tried so hard to learn to skate so she could show her dad the next time he comes home. She talked about Jasper nearly the entire time we skated. It's clear he's her hero, which is neat. But I don't know how she factors into Jenet and me. I mean, she's a huge factor and she comes with Jenet obviously, but our paths haven't crossed when I'm acting as Jenet's boyfriend. Fuck, is that what I am? My insides don't know if I should rejoice or ball up in the corner.

"It's way too soon to worry about that. You two haven't been seeing each other long enough for you to worry you may become a stepdad."

Shit. I hadn't even thought *that* far ahead. I was more concerned about the point where I'd eventually have to spend time with them both. Not the long away point after that where *if* things get real serious with Jenet, I'd be a father figure to the girl. Just the thought makes me sick. I'm not equipped. I'm in no shape to be a dad or stepdad, in this case. I'd suck. My past shows that in moments of need, I'm clearly no good.

"Cal," Collin starts as if he can tell I'm drowning in my own worries. "Stop. You can't keep running from what happened. Don't you want Wyatt to have cousins?"

Bastard. Using my nephew against me. If I have a weakness, it's him. In so many ways.

"You're good," Collin says when I don't say anything. "Have you given any more thought to seeing someone? Trace can recommend someone I'm sure."

Maybe I should. Even if things don't work out with Jenet, I'd like to see my nephew just once without a surge of pain hitting me smack in the chest.

"Get me a name, will you?"

"Absolutely," my twin replies with entirely too much eagerness. "Julie wants to do a double date with you and Jenet since things seem to be going well."

Of course she does. When she let the past go, she became too nice toward me. Even when I was dating Tori and she hated her, she was still nice for Collin and Wyatt's sake and invited us over.

"I'll ask." Doubtful I will, though. It's hard enough to see Jenet as it is outside of our runs. And with her moving, those will end. I don't want to share any more than I already have to.

We talk a bit longer before we hang up and I find a movie to watch while I draw. I check my phone to see if there's a text from Jenet. I messaged her earlier. Just to check in, you know. Make sure that bedtime with Caroline went okay—I couldn't think of anything else to send. She hasn't responded yet.

Maybe she's still busy with Caroline. Hopefully she isn't full of regret now that she's away from me and the sexual tension has chilled between us. That would be a hit to the chest I don't think I'm prepared to deal with.

Yet it seems likely the longer time passes without a response back. Eventually, I fall asleep and hope I'll hear from her tomorrow.

———

My body jolts awake as repeated knocks on my door echo throughout my apartment, sending my sketchpad and pencil to the floor. Knocking is tame word, though. Whoever it is absolutely pounds on the door. Half asleep, I amble over to the door, peering through and frowning when I see a red-faced Jenet.

As fast as my hands can move, I unlock the door and swing it open. My brain can't process the scene before me. Jenet's face is blotchy and tear-streaked. A sleepy, red-eyed Caroline stands next to her. Both are in their pajamas.

"I'm sorry," Jenet begins. "I had to get out of there. I didn't know where else to go. I didn't want to wake Julie at this time of night. Can we come in?"

Her question snaps me out of it and I move aside so they can enter my apartment. Struck silent, I follow Jenet as she leads Caroline to my bedroom. They both crawl in, hugging one another.

What the fuck is happening?

Jenet reaches her hand out behind her. I take that as my sign to climb in too. I want to ask questions, but if she hasn't said, it may be because of Caroline. They *both* begin to cry quietly.

What the hell?

She definitely came to the wrong home. I don't know what to do with them. One crying woman is bad enough; add a crying kid? Fuck me. Jenet has our hands linked and she pulls my arm until it's resting over the both of them.

I want to say it'll be okay. Find a way to reassure them both, but hell if I want to set them off further. With a slow and steady breath, I simply hold them close and doze off after both of them have.

In the morning, movement beneath my hand stirs me awake. I peel my eyes open just enough to see Caroline carefully moving away from Jenet. Caroline freezes when she's freed herself and sees me watching.

"I'm hungry," she whispers.

I slowly pull myself away from Jenet and wave for Caroline to follow me.

"You like pancakes, kid?" I ask once we're in the kitchen. She nods and rubs her swollen eyes. "Want to sit on the counter and help?" After a beat of hesitation, she nods. I pick her up and set her on the counter. Her eyes burn holes in my body as I gather what we need and then make my way back to her.

She watches as I measure and she dumps the mix and water into the bowl. She declines to stir, which is fine, and within a few minutes, a couple of pancakes cook on my stovetop.

When I glance over at her, her lower lip trembles and tears fall. Fuck.

"Is it really true?" she asks.

"Is what true?"

"That my daddy is an angel and can't come home?"

Fuck. Fuck. Fuck. Jasper died?

"Is that what your mom said?" I ask slowly.

Caroline nods. "I don't want him to be an angel in Heaven. Mommy said we can't visit people in Heaven because it's too far away."

"I'm sorry, Caroline." And I am. Immensely. How does a five-year-old even deal with death?

"I want my daddy," she cries. "He said he was coming home in three sleeps. He can't break a promise."

"I'm sorry he's not here," I tell her softly. There's got to be a way to soothe her. After a beat, I ask, "Do you know what happens to someone when they become an angel and there was someone they loved a whole, whole lot?" Caroline shakes her head. "They become guardian angels."

"What's that?"

"I bet your dad is a guardian angel. Yours. Because he loved you so much. So, even though you can't see or talk to him, he's still around, looking over you and protecting you because of how much he loved you. And because of how much you loved him. He's still in here." I press a finger to her chest.

"My daddy is a guarding angel?" she asks, seeming to seriously contemplate what I've told her.

I smile at her pronunciation and nod. "He sure is."

Caroline's tears stop and she watches me make pancakes. But then, her voice cracks as she asks, "Is Mommy going to leave and become my guarding angel too?"

"No, kid. I promise your mom isn't going anywhere." And I hope like hell I'm not lying to her. Surely, life wouldn't be so cruel as to take both parents before she's grown. Caroline seems satisfied with my answer.

By the time I've finished, Jenet walks into the kitchen. She mouths *thank you* for some reason and checks on Caroline who now happily eats her breakfast.

This is so far out of my wheelhouse, it's not even funny.

"Can I talk to you for a moment, Cal?"

Reluctantly, I nod and follow her back to my bedroom.

"I'm so sorry we barged in, but we found out Jasper died in a training accident and it felt so suffocating being in that house." Jenet groans. "We're supposed to move out tomorrow; his parents will be even more devastated." She takes a deep breath as more tears threaten to fall. "I'm sorry, Cal."

I find myself pulling her into a hug. "Don't be. I'm sorry about Jasper. I have to head out of here after a shower. I'll leave my key and get my spare from Collin. Stay as long as you need."

"Thank you," she mumbles into my chest.

I release her, she walks back to the kitchen, and I get ready.

The moment Collin sees me when I arrive for practice, he pulls me aside and asks, "What's wrong?"

I pace. "Jasper died. Jenet and Caroline showed up last night and climbed into my bed. I had to make Caroline breakfast this morning. This is too much. We've been on three dates, Collin, and she crashed at my apartment with her *daughter* because her ex-husband died. Why are you on your phone?" I snap.

"Letting Julie know so she can reach out to Jenet. On the bright side, you're already a safe place for her to land when shit hits the fan."

I grumble under my breath and walk away. Don't get me wrong, I like that Jenet sought me out. I just can't help but feel as if she's reaching out to the absolute worst person possible.

———

I couldn't even escape from my life at the game because they had a moment of silence for the service members who passed. It's a nice gesture, but all it did was cloud my mind while I played. Wondering how Jenet and Caroline are doing. Wondering if they're still at my place and what the fuck I'll do if they are.

When I get home, my apartment isn't quiet. I hear the TV in my room playing softly. I knew she'd be here. I saw her text after the game. I'm wholly unprepared, however, for how I feel when I walk into my bedroom to see the two of them snuggled together in the middle of the bed.

Is this what it's like to come home to someone? Tori slept in my bed, sure, but I never gave her access to my apartment so she could be here when I got home. This is new.

I...like it?

I grab some clothes and then disappear into the bathroom to change and finish getting ready for bed. Jenet has rolled over, her eyes open, when I return. I pause when I spot my sketchpad on the nightstand. Fuck. If I hide it now, will she ask questions or take that as a clear sign not to mention it?

My insides twist as I decide to ignore it and hope she follows suit. Once I've climbed in next to her, she snuggles against me.

"I'm sorry to invade your space again," she whispers. "He was my best friend and it breaks my heart that Caroline will never see him again. She told me you said he was her guardian angel; thank you for that. I think it's made it a little easier for her."

"I don't mind," I reply. Despite my freak-out this morning, it's true.

"His parents are so upset about us moving, but it was time and Jasper...being gone doesn't change anything."

"Do you need help moving?" I ask.

"Greg and Owen are helping; thank you, though."

Don't like that, but I don't have a real reason, so I keep quiet. My gaze wanders over to Caroline. She's sprawled out over half the bed. For such a little thing, she takes up a lot of room. It's kinda cute?

"She okay?" I can't help but ask. Her dad is gone and she's staying at a stranger's house. It's a stupid question.

"I guess? I kept her home from school today; she's been pretty quiet. I'm going to focus on her one hundred percent for a while; make sure she grieves okay."

Does that mean I'll see her even less? I don't want to ask. I don't want to be selfish again. "That sounds like a good plan," I say instead.

"Thank you, Cal."

I have no idea why she's thanking me. I pull her closer and fall asleep with what feels like the whole world in my arms.

# CHAPTER 8

## JENET

"How are you two doing?" Julie asks from where she sits on the bench next to me. The kids are only a few feet away, listening as a librarian reads them a story.

I sigh. "I don't know. It still doesn't feel real, to be honest. She seems okay. Her grandparents keep her after school and I think that's helped with the transition to our own place and dealing with Jasper being gone."

Julie nods. "How are things with Cal? I was hoping we could do a double date at some point."

"That sounds nice; I haven't seen him in what? Two weeks now, I think." Our schedules haven't aligned and honestly, I haven't tried too hard. Caroline just lost her dad. I don't want to leave her too much. "He calls me almost every night, though."

Julie eyes me for a moment and then says, "I think you're the one."

"The one what?"

"*The one*. The one to make him settle down."

I frown. "Didn't he date a girl for like three years before me?"

Julie waves her hand and rolls her eyes. "Yeah, but she was safe for him and he didn't care one way or the other about her. You, though? You'll help him overcome his demons and get him to settle down finally."

"Demons? What demons?" Not once has Cal made out like he has anything that troubles him. Well, maybe the fact that his career will end one day and he will feel lost at that point.

There's also the fact that he draws and not once has he mentioned that. I found his sketchpad on the floor, open to a drawing of me. My fingers flipped through the pages before I could think better of it. There were a ton of drawings of me. Enough that I wasn't sure if I should be flattered or worried.

There were also drawings of landscapes, wildlife, and the hockey arena. I placed it in his room and promised myself not to snoop further. When Cal saw it and froze, his muscles tenser than I've ever seen, I decided not to bring it up.

And I haven't.

It's a miracle.

"That's for him to share when he's ready," Julie answers, bringing me back to the present.

"Does Cal have any hobbies or interests outside of hockey?" I can't help but ask. Is it just me that doesn't know or everyone?

Julie snorts. "I wish he and Collin both did, but no."

That conversation with Julie stays on my mind all day. What could've marred Cal? He seems perfectly fine. Nothing seems to set him off. I just don't know. And why doesn't anyone know about his drawings? He's good. So freaking good.

"Mommy?"

"Yeah, honey?" I ask as I tuck Caroline into bed.

"Can we talk to guarding angels? Like, can I tell Daddy about my day?"

"Daddy already knows, but if you want to talk to him, I'm

sure he'd like that. Just close your eyes, think of him, and say whatever you want to say. He can't talk back, though, okay?"

She nods, quickly closes her eyes, and tells her daddy about a boy who pushed her today and other things that happened at school. I sit next to her and let her talk. I don't know if this is good or bad, but if it helps her, I won't take it away.

About five minutes and a goodnight later, she opens her eyes. "Night, Mommy."

"Night, hon."

I kiss her forehead and close her door as I leave. My phone vibrates with a text. I smile when I see it's from Cal. He's asking where I live, which is a bit weird, but Cal is a secret romantic. It may be a secret to him most of all. He sent flowers to my office last week. I got chocolate covered fruit earlier this week. Yesterday, he sent a gorgeous bracelet. All with little notes that he's thinking of me and misses me.

A knock on my door startles me out of my tidying thirty minutes later. I peer through the peephole and exhale a heavy breath.

"Cal, what are you doing here?" I ask as I open the door.

"I wanted to see you."

He steps inside and I realize he has a small duffel with him. Before I can protest, the duffel hits the floor, the door closes with a soft thud, and his hands cup my face. My knees weaken with his kiss. It's needy and desperate. A fire blazes in my body.

This is what's so dangerous about Cal. With minimal effort, he can play my body as he pleases and I love every minute of it. It's easy to forget even the most basic of things when he touches me.

"Cal," I breathe.

"I'll behave," he promises.

"Doesn't feel like you are." I barely contain my moan as his mouth attacks my neck and his hands find my breasts.

"Just give me a minute."

"Didn't take you for a minute man."

He laughs and lifts his head to finally—and unfortunately—stop his wonderful assault. "Sorry for barging in, but I needed to see you. What time does Caroline normally wake up?"

His change of topic confuses me for a moment. "Seven fifteen."

"I'll be out of here by six to be safe if you'll let me stay. I'll behave," he repeats. His head dips again to kiss me. My hands fist his shirt to keep from sliding to the floor. Good lord. This man. "Please?" he murmurs against my mouth.

Never did I expect a man like Cal to say please. It obliterates any protest immediately.

"Okay," I reply.

Cal grins, grabs his bag, and takes my hand. "Let's lay down."

As we walk back to my bedroom, I realize I'm in a ratty pair of sweats and a T-shirt that has at least three holes in it. Cal didn't seem to notice. At least, I hope he didn't. I sneak off to my bathroom in hopes of making myself look a bit more presentable. When I return, thoughts of behaving fly out of my mind. Cal sits in the middle of my bed, shirtless. To make sure she doesn't walk in during the night, I lock my door before climbing into bed.

Cal quickly grabs my hips and has me straddle him. Before I can say anything, he cups the back of my neck and kisses me. My hands can't help but brace on his wonderful chest.

"Missed you," he murmurs. His hands begin to roam again and I struggle to remember why we're supposed to behave. Cal presses his face to my neck and sighs. "Fuck, you feel like coming home and I'm obsessed."

My entire body literally swoons. "See, you say stuff like that and I forget about the red flags."

He laughs. "I still have red flags?"

"Tons. I'm thinking you lied about knowing how to date."

Cal just chuckles. He reaches over to grab his phone off the nightstand.

"What are you doing?" I ask.

"Setting my alarm before I forget." He does and then tosses his phone back on the nightstand. "One more minute, maybe twenty, and then we'll go to sleep, I swear." His hands slip beneath my shirt and his mouth crashes into mine once more.

My hips rock against him. When was the last time we even had sex? Not recent enough.

"Cal," I say through a half moan, half groan as his hands grab my ass and help me rock.

He sighs. "Right. Behaving. Sorry."

I shake my head. "No behaving. I missed you too." Before I can change my mind, I remove my shirt.

"Are you sure?" he asks.

In answer, I lean forward and kiss him. He's impossible to resist when he's half naked, it's been weeks since we were last intimate, and he's so damn sweet. I'm absolutely sure.

———

If Cal is in town, he shows up at my house once Caroline is in bed and he's always gone the next morning way before she wakes up. I don't mind one bit. It's nice to see him and being able to have sex regularly is wonderful too.

Julie and I are once again at the library for a little craft session they are having for Valentine's Day when my phone vibrates with a text from Cal.

CAL

We need to go out like normal people.
Starting to feel dirty, slinking in and out of
your house during the night. We can't miss
doing something for Valentine's Day.

Tomorrow? Caroline can come. We can go
see a movie or whatever five-year-olds like.

"Wow," Julie breathes from next to me and I quickly realize she's peering over at my text. "Never thought that'd happen."

"What? That he wants to spend time with Caroline?" I frown at the thought. He's known from the beginning that we're a package deal.

"Not that; that he'd ask for more. He's settling down," she finishes with a grin.

"Do you think it's too soon to officially introduce them?"

Julie sighs. "I've never been in your position, Jenet. Only you can decide that, I think."

The problem is, I'm not sure I'm thinking clear enough to make that decision. When I apparently don't respond soon enough for Cal, I get another text.

CAL

I'll be just a hockey player, if you want. We
can take her skating again.

I don't understand why Cal thinks he's an asshole. He's the most considerate person I've ever met.

JENET

It's a date. There's a movie she wants to see
if you're okay with that?

CAL

As long as I get to see you, I don't care what
we do.

And that is how the next night, I find myself anxiously waiting for Cal to pick us up.

"Hon," I start when Caroline runs into my room to watch me get ready. "You know that movie you want to see?" She nods. "And you remember Cal?" She nods again. "He's going to take us to see it."

"Okay."

I've never gotten this far with a man and I'm unsure if I should say more. I realize now that maybe I should have laid down some rules with Cal too. With a sigh, I realize she's without shoes.

"Will you put your shoes on for me?"

Caroline runs out of the room without answering. I give myself a once-over. There's nothing fancy about my outfit. Just a cute pair of boots, jeans, and a sweater. I did throw some earrings on and curled my hair a little. My hands tremble and I take a deep breath to settle my nerves as the doorbell chimes.

"He's here!" Caroline shouts.

I laugh a little and follow after her. She stands next to me as I open the door.

My breath catches as I take in Cal in just jeans and long-sleeved shirt. That same white beanie is on his head. But what makes my heart stutter is that he holds two bouquets of flowers. Both are the same size, but one has all pink flowers and the other has a variety of colors.

"Hey," he says, snapping me out of my amazement. His gaze drops and he adds, "Hey, kid. I brought flowers for you and your mom."

I look down just in time to see her eyes light up. She immediately goes for the bouquet with the pink flowers and gives them a healthy sniff.

"Thank you!" she chirps. Caroline looks up at me. "Mommy, look!"

"I see. Let's put them in some water before we go."

Cal steps into the house and I manage to find two vases. Once I have the flowers in the vases, Caroline insists that hers should be in her room, so we place them in there before leaving. It's not until we get into the car that I realize Cal has a nervous energy about him.

I want to say something without addressing it. Before I can, Cal asks Caroline, "What's your favorite movie snack, kid? Popcorn?"

Part of me wants to bristle at him calling her kid instead of her name, but I'm certain he doesn't mean anything by it. His question spurs Caroline to list all her favorite movie snacks.

"Popcorn, M&Ms, and gummy bears. But Mommy only ever lets me choose one." She sighs as if it's such an unfair hardship.

"What about you?" he asks.

"Popcorn and SnoCaps with a Coke slushy."

"Do you only get to choose one too?" he teases.

"No!" Caroline tattles, clearly outraged we don't have the same rules.

Cal laughs. Within a few minutes, we've arrived at the movie theater. As we walk inside, Cal grabs my hand, but quickly releases it with an apologetic look. That alone makes me want to grab his hand. But Caroline has never seen me with anyone and I'm still a bit nervous about making it obvious to my daughter that Cal may be coming around more often.

"Tonight is a special night," Cal says when we get in the line for concessions. He looks down at Caroline with a smile. "Just this once, you can get as many snacks as you want."

She immediately looks at me with wide eyes. "Really?"

I want to say no because she doesn't need all the junk and because she certainly won't consume everything, but I don't want to turn Cal down either, so I nod. Caroline releases a little squeal before facing the rows of candy. She even presses her face to the glass as she thinks about what she wants.

While we wait for her, Cal orders my favorite snacks and then says to my daughter, "All right, kid. What's it going to be?"

"A slushy like Mommy, my *own* popcorn, and these." She proceeds to point to three different boxes of candy. Cal nods at the attendant who gets to work on her request after I cut in to make it a small slushy and a small popcorn.

With that settled, we make our way to the movie theater. Caroline and I end up backtracking for the bathroom. She actually does pretty good with movies, which is the only reason I take her. We settle into our seats and because I can't help myself, I reach over and discreetly take Cal's hand.

I nearly laugh. It's like I'm back in school, trying to be sneaky with a boy. Cal squeezes my hand and seems to finally relax. We watch the movie about a family of ducks. Caroline does about like I expected and really only has a few of each of the candies. She wipes out most of her popcorn and drink, though.

When the movie ends and the lights come back on, Cal leans forward to address Caroline.

"Did you like it?" She nods and then he asks, "Favorite place to eat? I'm starved."

Caroline seems to seriously consider it, but she only has one favorite place.

"The chip place."

Cal flicks his glance to me in confusion.

"There's a Mexican restaurant across town. That's what she's talking about."

He nods and then off we go. Cal does well balancing questions between the two of us as we eat dinner. It's nice to see this side of him, though I'm not surprised. Not after watching him skate with her and then with what Caroline said he told her about Jasper being her guardian angel.

Caroline falls asleep on the way home. Cal unlocks my

door for me as I carry her inside and get her to bed. I find him on the couch with his head in his hands afterward.

"Everything okay?"

He jerks up and gives me an easy smile. "Yeah. Thanks for letting her be around me so I could spend time with you."

"Thanks for making it an easy decision." I take a seat next to him and rest my head on his shoulder.

"I've never gone out for Valentine's Day with a woman, much less with a kid in tow."

"Red flag number three thirty-four," I reply immediately. Cal laughs. "I'm serious," I tease as I sit up. "You dated a woman for three years; you never took her out for Valentine's Day?"

A blush colors his cheeks. "Dated may have been a strong word," he admits.

"How did you break up with her?" I ask, now curious about how he treated this woman.

Cal immediately shakes his head. "I don't want to answer that."

When I raise a brow and say, "That'll be another red flag," he counters with, "If I answer, it'll probably be one too. I'm in a lose-lose situation."

Well, now I'm super curious, so I stare at him to wait him out. It works. Within two minutes, he reluctantly tells me, "Over a text. She didn't care, though. Her response was basically, okay. Suit yourself."

"So, it was really an extended friends with benefits type thing."

Cal shrugs. "Friends may be a strong word too."

I can't help it; I laugh. He had a fuck buddy for three years and called it a relationship.

"Are you done searching for my red flags?" he asks.

"Maybe."

He grabs my hand and tugs just enough to let me know

what he wants. "I'll behave," he promises before I can voice an answer either way. "Just need to feel you," he adds softly.

He's impossible to resist. He tugs again and I move to straddle his lap. His hands immediately roam. Over my thighs, up my back, through my hair, over my chest. Cal shakes his head in bewilderment. He ducks and begins kissing and nipping at my neck. I grab his shoulders and hold on. I already know my willpower is low where Cal is concerned.

"You feel amazing," he mutters against my skin between kisses. "I've never..."

When a minute goes by without him finishing his sentence, I prod, "Never what?"

Cal deflects further by pressing a hard kiss to my mouth. It's easy to follow his lead. When his hands squeeze my breasts, I remember his unfinished sentence.

I pull away and grasp his face. "Never what, Cal?" I ask softly.

He sighs, but doesn't shy away thankfully. "You feel like home." He's said this before. "I've never felt that with someone. Felt so at peace and content and like you're a place to land amongst all the bullshit."

This surprises me. That he feels this way. Cal hasn't turned to me in a moment of distress. There hasn't been been anything that's happened where I felt like he confided in me about something serious. So while I appreciate his comment, I don't understand it.

"Why?"

Cal shakes his head. "Don't know."

"I want to ask you something, but I don't want you to feel pressured to respond if you don't want to."

He says nothing, appearing relaxed. However, the tips of his fingers dig into my hips where they now rest. He lifts his chin to silently urge me forward.

"Why is your drawing ability a secret?"

His muscles coil so tightly so suddenly that I regret asking.

"Never mind," I hurry to say. "Just…I hope you'll tell me one day."

We fall into an awkward silence until Cal tentatively asks, "Can I stay?"

In answer, I stand. Cal follows me to my room where I put on *Lords of the Rings*. I keep falling asleep before we can finish the first movie; Cal doesn't seem to mind. But Cal, with just his fingertips moving innocently over my body, distracts me until I'm pulling our clothes off.

Tonight seems different than others. Cal normally attacks with a hunger. A desperation. But tonight, he kisses and touches me as if he has all night long. It feels an awful lot like he's making love, but I shove that thought away and focus on how he makes me feel right now.

Cherished.

Treasured.

Worshiped.

Like I'm his whole world.

A shiver runs through me and Cal grins.

"Fucking perfect." That's all he's said since we entered my room and I can't help but think the same thing about him.

# CHAPTER 9

## CAL

Ever since Jenet let me take the two of them on a date, I've been able to spend more time with her. Granted, I'm also spending time with Caroline, but it's been worth it. She's got me twisted up enough that after Collin's therapist recommended someone, I've been seeing her.

I hate every second of it. I don't like she's a woman and I have zero rights to feel this way. At the same time, I feel like I'm at my wits' end. This thing with Jenet drives me crazy. Half the time she feels like exactly where I need to be and the other time, I want to run far away. Julie and Collin seem to think this will help, so I'm trying.

Right now, though, I've stopped by Jenet's place today for dinner. Caroline sits on the porch steps, looking rather sad.

"What's up, kid?" I ask.

"T-ball started, but Daddy isn't here to help me practice."

"He threw the ball with you?"

Caroline nods. "He played and said he would teach me." Her eyes seem to light up and she says, "Will you throw the ball to me? Mommy said she couldn't because she's cooking. Please?"

"I'm a hockey player, Caroline. Don't think I'm too good

at baseball." Her shoulders slump. Fuck me. If I can't say no to Jenet, I sure as hell can't say no to her daughter. "But we can give it a go. Just take it easy on me."

She lights up with my change of heart and jumps up. "Okay!"

And that's how I find myself tossing a ball with a kid. She enjoys my theatrics about how fast and hard she throws, especially because she keeps telling me she's taking it easy on me. It's easy to make her laugh. I *like* making her laugh. Caroline is a pretty great kid. I'm not saying I want to be a dad or anything, but it's getting easier to be around both her and Wyatt.

"Okay," she says about thirty minutes later. "This one will be *really* fast. Do you want my glove?"

I laugh and shake my head. "Give me your best."

She takes a big breath. She throws the ball, but releases early. It soars high. I jog backward, but it's no use. The ball hits the hood of my vehicle with a loud thunk. It leaves a decent dent and I hear a sharp gasp behind me.

"I'm so sorry!" Caroline screams as she runs over. "Did I hurt your car? I didn't mean to! I swear!"

For some reason, all I can do is laugh. I glance down at Caroline. "Kid, you didn't tell me your dad gave you his throwing arm and all that power."

Caroline is confused for a moment, but then she smiles. "I got that from Daddy?"

"Must've," I confirm.

Her smile is huge, but then it falters as she glances over at my car. She lifts on her tippy toes as if that'll help her see the hood and the damage. "You aren't mad?"

I shake my head. "Just a car, Caroline, and you didn't mean it. I can get it fixed." I shrug. "We should probably call it a day and check on your mom."

When I turn around, Jenet's on the steps, smiling. Caroline runs over, talking a hundred miles an hour to tell her what happened. Jenet ushers her inside once she's done and then throws me another smile.

"You are fantastic, you know that?"

"What makes you say that?"

"You're so sweet to her."

I frown. Am I, really? I don't think I'm sweet. "Just being nice like a normal person."

"Thank you," she says, disregarding what I said.

This topic makes me uncomfortable, so I give her a quick kiss and walk inside to end the conversation. I want to soak up all the time I can. Hockey is about to get crazy with the playoffs starting soon.

"Do you want to come to one of my games?" Caroline asks over dinner.

"Honey, his schedule is pretty busy with hockey," Jenet cuts in.

"But I can try if you want me to come," I add, earning a big grin from Caroline who nods.

"Can we go to another one of your games?" she asks.

"If you and your mom want."

Caroline looks at Jenet who nods. It's almost as if in that moment, my brain believes I have Caroline's approval. That's the craziest thing I've felt so far, but I don't overthink it. I just let it be.

———

Julie doesn't get her double date, but we do manage to find time to go to their place for dinner. Julie and Jenet are tucked away in the kitchen, gossiping I'm sure. Wyatt lies on Collin's chest from where they sit on the couch. He seems worn out and ready to fall asleep at any moment.

Caroline walks over to me after getting something to drink in the kitchen.

"Can I sit with you?" she asks.

I freeze in my place in Collin's recliner. I find myself nodding as I wonder if she's feeling shy around Collin with Wyatt too tired to play. She climbs onto my lap and then rests her head on my shoulder to watch whatever stupid fucking kid's show Collin has playing on the TV.

Collin snorts and I glare when I realize he's laughing at me and my discomfort.

"You worry and punish yourself too much," he says.

I shush him because I don't trust my voice and we absolutely do not need to talk about this in front of Caroline. Her little ears are always listening.

"There's nothing wrong with moving on and being happy," Collin adds.

I give him no reaction. Maybe if I ignore him, he'll shut the fuck up.

"Cal?" Caroline says a few minutes later.

"Yeah, kid?"

"Can we get ice cream before we go home?"

This girl loves her treats. She has started asking me because we both realized at some point that I never say no to her. I literally have no idea how Jenet does it. Caroline doesn't even have to look at me with those big eyes of her. I still say yes.

It drives Jenet crazy. Caroline got a toy out of me once when just before some road games, I went with Jenet and Caroline grocery shopping. I didn't know Caroline had asked Jenet the last time they were in the store for the little toy and when she asked me, I agreed without even thinking.

So in efforts to keep Jenet happy, I reply with, "Only if your mom says we can."

Caroline sighs. "She said no."

I laugh. "You already asked her?" After she nods, I ask, "Are you trying to get me in trouble? Your mom would've been upset with us both if I said yes when she already told you no."

This is Caroline's new thing. Asking me after asking her mom.

Caroline sits up with wide eyes. "Mommy will be mad?"

"She won't be happy," I confirm.

"Oh. I'm sorry."

"It's okay."

When she makes a comment about being hungry, I encourage her to check with her mom on when we're eating.

"You're a natural," Collin says.

"If you don't shut up, we're leaving," I warn. "I don't want to talk about this with you and certainly not with Jenet and Caroline in the house."

Collin takes me seriously finally and shuts up. It's easy to be around Jenet and Caroline and forget about my issues when we're at her house and it's just the three of us. Being around my brother and his family remind me of what I've been trying to forget.

My therapist tells me there's nothing to forgive. I made a decision. Regretted it. There was no actual harm done. Everyone has moved on. I should too. It's not nearly that simple, but being with Jenet helps.

My therapist thinks so too because she wants me to tell Jenet about what happened with Julie. I don't see the point. It's a hard no. She thinks it'll be cathartic. I think it'll be massively stupid. There's no reason for Jenet to know about my past. Especially since I'm working on overcoming it.

I zone out a bit during our time at Collin's. That horrible buzzing energy distracts me too much. It numbs me. It worries me. We drop Caroline off at her grandparents' for a sleepover and then we return to my apartment.

That energy eats away at my gut. It's impossible to ignore. Not even sex with Jenet eases it. Once she falls asleep, I slip out of bed and leave a note just in case. I don't want to freak her out if she wakes up but I hope to god she doesn't wake up.

I escape my apartment and go into the one next door. Canvases are scattered everywhere, but I ignore them. Well, all but one. A three-foot-by-three-foot canvas rests on my easel. Jenet's eyes haunt me in the best possible way and when it comes to painting, that's the only thing I can paint lately.

There are half a dozen unfinished canvases of just her eyes. I can't get the color right. I'm close, though. Once my supplies are ready, I shove all the unwanted thoughts and feelings down and paint.

The colors don't fall together like I want, pissing me off, so I place it aside and work on something else that will likely never see the light of day. I overheard Caroline last week mentioning to Jenet about how she misses her dad and if she was sure her guarding angel couldn't come down to give her a hug.

Ever since, I haven't been able to get rid of this...this need. So I've been working on something for her. She'll never get it, but I've been working on it. I doubt if I did give it to her, she'd like it. Doesn't matter.

The painting is of her and her dad on a ball field, throwing the ball to one another. Jasper never got the chance. It seemed like a nice thought. I certainly wish he was here for her.

Time passes and with each stroke of the brush, my muscles uncoil and that toxic energy dissipates. My chest labors with ease. My shoulders relax. With a sigh of relief, I set the paintbrush down, finally tired.

"Red flag number five sixty-one."

I whirl around at the sound of Jenet's voice, all that tension flooding my system again. She can't be here. Jenet, with only my T-shirt on, steps further into the apartment and soaks in my work.

"And five sixty-two," she adds as she comes to a stop next to me. "What's with all the eyes? It's a little creepy."

At this, I can't help but force a laugh. "It's your eyes. Well, supposed to be."

She grabs my arm as she takes in the canvas on the easel. "Is that Caroline and Jasper?" she asks with watery eyes.

"Yeah. Let's go." Her mouth opens, but I shake my head. "Not today, Jenet. Forget everything you've seen."

She frowns. "Please?"

"No."

I grab her elbow, lead her out of the apartment, lock it up and finally return to bed to get some sleep. Jenet's disappointment is obvious, but I don't care. I've given her a lot. I've given *Caroline* a lot. Sharing this part of myself isn't possible right now.

―――――

It doesn't seem as if Jenet gets pampered a lot, so I tend to do things that will be a treat for her. We were supposed to get massages again today and do a few other relaxing things, but Jenet called earlier to cancel. Caroline was supposed to be with her grandparents while we went out, but both are feeling a bit under the weather.

No big deal. I want to see Jenet today and that's exactly what I'm going to do.

"Cal! What are you doing here?" Jenet asks when she opens the door to me.

"We're going out."

"But I told you—"

"All three of us." Caroline appears next to Jenet and I look down at her. "Hey, kid. Can I hang with you and your mom today?"

She nods eagerly.

"Can you get your shoes on then?"

"Cal," Jenet starts as Caroline rushes off. I lift my gaze back to hers and she simply stares at me. She wants to protest for some reason, but is also deciding not to. "Okay," she replies with a nod. "Give us two minutes."

It takes ten, but then we're in Jenet's car and on our way. I tweaked our plans slightly and hope they'll still work. I should've cleared it with Jenet to make sure it's appropriate and something Caroline will enjoy.

"The nail place, Mommy!" Caroline shouts excitedly when I park outside of the nail salon.

"I see." Jenet looks over at me. "What are we doing here?"

"I figured you could both use some pampering."

Jenet blinks at me but Caroline speaks and we exit the car. The only thing I'm getting out of this is spending time with them. This day is about catering to them both. It's odd I don't mind. At least not in this moment.

The girls are ushered to a pair of seats where they'll get their feet done and then their hands. I sit in a chair within the waiting area with my phone in hand. Just need to wait this out until we go to the next place.

"Cal!"

My head snaps up at Caroline shouting across the room. She waves me over. I hesitantly walk to her.

"She said you could sit with us." She points at the seat next to her. "Now you don't have to be by yourself."

"Thanks, kid." I sit in the seat next to her and let my legs rest on the sides of the little tub. One of the ladies ask if I also want the little foot treatment. I can't say no fast enough, making the girls laugh.

"Are you coming to my birthday party?" Caroline asks me.

Jenet already told me about her party and how she let Caroline know I can't come. We have an away game. Caroline is bummed; I'm guessing she's asking in hopes of getting a different answer from me.

"Sorry, kid." Her little shoulders sag. I've never felt so horrible about missing something in my whole life. The feeling that I've let her down overwhelms me. "But I did get you something." Her eyes light up. "You have to wait until your party to get it, though. I'll leave it with your mom before I leave, so you'll have it."

Caroline talks my ears off while they get their nails done. I then take them to get their hair all dolled up. Jenet keeps giving me glances. Good glances, I think. Like she can't believe I'm doing this for them. I'm not really doing anything, though. Julie made the appointments for me since I wasn't sure where to go, especially with Caroline in tow. I'm just paying for it and hanging out while they enjoy themselves.

After they get their hair done, Caroline slips her hand through mine as we walk back to the car. That little action is huge. So huge, I don't know how to process. I shove the warm feeling down deep and look down at her.

"Do you like to shop, kid?"

"Cal—" Jenet starts.

"Yes!" Caroline interrupts to answer me.

"That's what we're doing next."

Caroline claps her hands and hops into the car. After Jenet buckles her in, she closes the door and folds her arms over her chest as she looks at me.

"You don't need to spend money on us all day. She'd be tickled going to the park to play."

"I don't mind."

Jenet huffs. "I know, but you're spoiling her."

I frown. "That's a bad thing? I just wanted to spend time with you and treat you both."

Her arms fall by her sides. The fight leaves her; I don't understand why it was there to begin with. "It's not a bad thing," she replies softly. "It's super sweet. I just don't want her to get used to this."

I nod, but I'm even more confused. Not used to spending time with me? Me treating them? Being pampered in general?

What doesn't she want her to get used to? I'm fucking this up, but I don't know how to stop.

"Cal, we appreciate it," Jenet says. "You just don't have to do this. Every time you're with us, you splurge."

I frown. It's not like I'm tossing thousands of dollars out on them.

"I'm not saying this right," Jenet says, clearly seeing my confusion.

"I only want to do something nice for you both. It's not a lot and I don't mind. I like doing it."

"I'm not used to this," she whispers.

I want to hug her but our contact around Caroline remains limited. I open her door and sneak in a kiss to her temple before she gets inside. "You should get used to it then."

# CHAPTER 10
## CAL

My heart beats in my chest. Game four. Round two. We have a chance to sweep. Fucking sweep! Then, it'll be on to round three. Jenet and Caroline are in the stands amongst an arena full of Rebels fans.

There's only five minutes left and we're up three to two. We just need to hold this lead for the next five minutes, bump this team out, and we're on to the next round. The seconds tick down beautifully. The other team gets a penalty and we're on a fucking power play with three minutes to go.

Collin and I race down the ice. He passes me the puck. It soars over, hitting my stick with a lovely thud. I swing my stick back. Within seconds, the puck flies through the air, slips right between the goalie's arm and torso, and the horn sounds.

If I could live here on cloud nine, I would. Adrenaline courses through my blood like a high. This right here, winning another game—a *playoff* game—and knowing we're advancing? It's one of the best feelings in the world. Like many other times, I feel unworthy of this moment. This feeling.

The war that wages within me causes me to take my time

to savor the positive feelings. I don't deserve this. To be here. But fuck if I'll let it go. All I want is to lift the Cup up one time. To dare dream of anything more would be greedy and selfish. To even want that dream seems like tempting fate. As if I'm asking for too much.

I manage to be one of the last to leave the arena. As I head out, I spot a group of fans standing around a vehicle with the hood up. I'm not sure if they are fans of the Rebels or not as they are surprisingly not wearing jerseys. Maybe they were fans of the other team and took them off after the game.

Since my asshole days are behind me, I stop and roll down my window.

"Need any help?" I ask.

"Hey! We just need a jump," the guy slurs.

They move out of the way and I pull my vehicle up closer to theirs. One of them makes a comment on who I am—one of the Kessy twins—and there are rumbles made amongst them.

"Do you have cables?" I ask. "If not, I have some."

"We don't."

I turn to head toward the back of my vehicle. Something is said, but I don't catch it before a sharp pain hits the back of my head. Dots flash over my vision as I'm swarmed and pain explodes all over my body.

I attempt to fight back, but I'm surrounded. Something hits my face, causing me to scream out and clutch my left side. My face is wet with blood as I fall to my knees, my vision disappearing on me.

I knew my current life was too good to be true. I wished for too much and now the powers that be are punishing me for it.

———

My tongue feels thick and my head fucking hurts. I peel my eyelids open and then frown. What the hell?

"Leave it alone," Collin says before my fingers reach my face to detect what's wrong with me. The pain and regret in his tone make me turn my head to look at him. Something covers my left eye and he's on my left side, so I have to turn my head more than I normally would.

"What happened? What's wrong?"

The look on Collin's face causes pure panic to swell within me. He looks like he's about to put an animal down or something. My fingers touch the bandage over my eye. Over half my face, really. What's wrong with me?

"Tell me!" I demand with a shout as terror floods my veins.

"I'm sorry," he whispers. "They think there'll be permanent vision loss in your left eye."

The room sways. I've lost half of my vision? Collin continues to talk and explain what happened to me—apparently I was jumped by five guys who stopped me as I was leaving the arena last night—and I nearly lost my fucking eye. I just lost half my sight instead.

The game—my *life*—is over. I can't play if I can't fucking see. What in the hell am I supposed to do now? We're on a path to the fucking Cup and it's out of my grasp forever. I was so damn close! The closest I've ever been. And just like that it's gone. It was my last chance and I had no fucking idea.

"Get out," I rasp. He can't be here; *I* don't want to be here. I'd rather be dead. Why couldn't they kill me? When Collin only stops talking and doesn't move, I scream, "GET OUT!"

"Cal," he starts.

I swing my legs over the bed as if I can actually stand; my body sways to prove I can't.

"Get the fuck out," I snarl. "I will throw you out if I have to."

"Cal?"

I squeeze my eyes closed and wince at the sound of her voice.

"Jenet, I don't—" Collin starts.

I stand but immediately fall back down onto the bed.

"Jesus, Cal," Collin says at the same time Jenet cautiously asks, "What's going on?"

"Get him out of here," I demand to her. If Collin doesn't want to leave willingly, then maybe I can get Jenet to make him.

Only the sound of my labored breathing fills the air before Jenet says, "I think you should go. I'll stay with him."

She won't. She's the next one to leave. Collin sighs, but walks out after making some asinine comment about how he's here if I need anything. What I need is my fucking sight.

"Come on. Let's get you settled back in bed," Jenet says softly. I let her help me and before I can ask her to leave too, she climbs in next to me. "Your world has fallen apart. Let me be here for you like you were there for me."

I squeeze my eye closed. How can I ask her to leave when she throws it in my face that I was there for her when Jasper died? I wasn't even there voluntarily. She gave me no choice when she showed up at my doorstep.

"What about Caroline?" I ask. Not because I care—at least I don't want to care—but because I'm hoping she'll be why Jenet has to leave.

"She's fine. She knows you're hurt and she's worried." She pauses. "Can you do me a big, quick favor?"

Those words out of Jenet's mouth are never a good thing. They always involve Caroline.

Still, I find myself warily asking, "What?"

"Can she see you?" When I tense next to her, she adds, "Her dad died after getting hurt, Cal. I've told her you're okay, but she thinks you're never coming back like Jasper." Jenet's voice catches in her throat and I want to scream.

All I want to do is absorb and wallow in the fact that my

life is over. I don't want to worry about some fucking kid who isn't even mine. Yet the image of how scared Caroline looked that morning after they showed up at my apartment pops up in my mind. I don't want her worried about me. With a sigh, I can only manage a, "Yeah."

"Can we do it now and get it over with?"

"She's here now?"

"In the waiting room with her grandma. She threw a tantrum of epic proportions when I was leaving the house to come see you and I told her I'd ask if you could have little visitors."

My hands clench in fists. I don't want to deal with this right now! "Go get her," I find myself saying like my mouth and brain aren't connected.

Jenet eases up, gives me a soft kiss, and then a minute later returns with a crying Caroline. Before I can even open my arms for her, she runs and launches onto the bed. I grunt at she throws herself at me, wailing.

"I'm okay, kid." I pat her back, feeling extremely awkward. Caroline has her arms locked as tight as she can around me and she cries into my neck.

After a moment, I realize she's talking. "Please don't die. I don't want you to go away like my daddy. Please don't die."

Unable to deny the urge to comfort her, I wrap my arms around her and hug her tight despite the pain that courses through my body. "I'm okay," I repeat. "I'll bust out of here soon." I'm not sure if that's true or not since I haven't seen a doctor. Is there anything to heal? "I'm not going anywhere, kid. Promise."

"Okay, Caroline. You've seen him. He's okay. Grandma's going to take you home now."

"No!" she screeches in my ear the moment Jenet touches her.

"Just leave her." Jenet looks like she wants to protest, but

I'm not in the mood to watch Caroline get upset over having to leave. "I'm tired, kid. You okay if I take a nap?"

She nods against my neck and I close my eyes, unable to fight the exhaustion any longer.

"Let me at least move her to the chair," Jenet says, but I wave her off.

Caroline relaxes against me finally and loosens her grip. I'm not sure which of us falls asleep first. Maybe she'll be the only one who'll wake up.

# CHAPTER 11

## JENET

When Cal didn't show up after the game as promised, I panicked. I called Julie who told Collin. Collin circled back to the arena and found Cal bleeding like crazy on the ground. He had been worked over pretty good, but when Collin told me about his face, I really started to worry.

For good reason too. Those bastards who attacked him slashed up his face, broke bones in his face, and took his eyesight in his left eye. At least, the doctors think it's highly likely after seeing the damage. Cal was unconscious for three days before he woke up yesterday. As soon as Collin texted me, I hauled ass to the hospital.

I was in the middle of picking up Caroline. It's been difficult to act as if things are normal, but I didn't want to worry her yet. When Collin called, it was hard to contain myself. I finally broke down to tell her that Cal had been hurt and he was in the hospital where doctors could look after him.

What I wasn't expecting was Caroline's reaction to that. She immediately started crying, even though I reassured her he was okay. When she realized I was heading to Carol's to drop her off, she lost her mind, insisting she had to see Cal too.

So off to the hospital we went with Carol on her way to take her home. That didn't happen, though. Cal surprised me by letting Caroline stay.

Now, they both sleep snuggled together in the hospital bed. Half of Cal's face is covered with gauze, but with only half of his face exposed, it's clear he's upset even in his sleep. I gently shake Caroline's shoulder.

I place a finger over my mouth in a silent request that she stay quiet. "Grandma is here to take you home to get ready for school." At her frown, I say, "He's okay, but we need to let him rest and heal so he can come home."

Caroline nods and allows me to help her out of the bed. We meet Carol and I see her off. When I return to Cal's room, his eyes are open, but they stare lifelessly at the wall across from him.

"Need anything?" I ask softly.

His hands form fists, but he otherwise doesn't respond. After about two hours of silence, he speaks.

"You don't need to be here."

I jerk back in surprise. "Cal," I start, ready to protest that outrageous statement.

"Don't you need to work?" he interrupts.

"It can wait."

"There's nothing to do here and I don't need a babysitter. You can go." His voice is flat. Emotionless.

There's a knock on his door and a woman pokes her head in.

"Can I come in?" she asks.

When I glance at Cal, his features harden. "Go away, Sylvia. There's nothing to gossip about here."

I have no idea who this woman is but Cal's comment hurts her based on the expression on her face.

"Cal, we just want to check on you."

"Jenet, you can stay if you make sure I have no visitors. Not even my brother." When I open my mouth to protest, he cuts me a look so full of anger, it steals my breath. "Either keep everyone away or leave."

"I'll go," Sylvia pipes up. "Can I talk to you for a second, Jenet?"

Cal doesn't seem to care one way or another, so I stand and follow her out of the room.

"Sylvia Boyd," she says with an outstretched hand. "My husband plays with the Rebels, too. We'll give him some space, but I wanted your number. In case there's anything either of you needs."

"Oh. Thank you."

We exchange numbers. Sylvia gives me a hug and then she's gone. Julie rounds the corner a moment later with Wyatt. I shake my head before she can get too close.

"He doesn't want to see anyone. He threatened to kick me out if I let anyone in to see him," I say once she's close enough. "He doesn't even want Collin coming back."

Her shoulders slump. "Do you need anything?"

I shake my head.

"Okay; let me know. Between Sylvia and me, we'll let everyone else know not to visit."

"Thanks."

She gives me a quick hug and then off they go. When I step back into Cal's room, there's the briefest of gratefulness in his glance before he shuts it down and looks away.

It breaks my heart that he's experiencing this. Even more so that his career has ended. Cal's living his worst fear. I don't know how to help him with this. I don't know what to say. Nothing will make it easier for him to absorb. Not right now.

———

A few more days pass where I spend my days at the hospital and my nights at home with Caroline. Cal gets discharged today and there's no way I could miss that. Collin already brought his car to his complex. Meanwhile, Cal shuns anyone related to the Rebels. His parents have even called and he refuses to talk to them, too. At this point, I feel lucky he's letting me stick around.

I tried to convince him to stay with me, but he answered with a hard no, followed by how he didn't want Caroline to see him like this. She wouldn't care as long as he was there and okay, but I didn't push harder.

The moment we stop outside of his apartment door, Cal turns toward me with a sigh.

"I just want to be alone, Jenet. Can you please do that?"

The please is what does me in. That and the jagged scars down his face. I wasn't quite prepared for when they removed the bandages. He has three scars on the side of his face and his eyelid now remains closed. He tried to open it and was unable.

"You'll let me come back?" I ask. That's my biggest worry. That he'll push me away too and stay here to wallow in his despair.

An agonizing minute passes before he nods. I want to hug him, but I don't want to upset him further either. Why that would upset him, I don't know, but this isn't a Cal I'm familiar with and that makes me hesitate.

Cal must sense I'm waiting for something because he opens his arms for me. I hurry over, hug him hard despite any pain I may cause, and whisper, "I'm here. Please don't push me away forever."

He doesn't respond. His arms flex once before he releases me. He unlocks his apartment door and steps inside without another look.

My heart fractures in that moment. Why do I feel like I just lost him?

# CHAPTER 12
## CAL

Finally discharged from the hospital, I return home to my apartment with no plans to ever leave again. The only minor temptation I have is to maybe go back home to Florida. But that would take more effort than I care to exert at the moment.

Despite being clear I don't want to see anyone, the Rebels women knock on my door seemingly all the time. I never let anyone in. The last thing I want to do is see anyone or anything related to *that*.

Jenet has stopped by too. I don't want to see her either, but she ignores me when I tell her I don't want her here. I'm too weak when it comes to her to actually toss her out. My mind is swamped with regret. The list of all the things I did in the name of hockey constantly filter through my mind.

I walked away from a possible baby.

I carelessly dated, not wanting to get bogged down by anyone.

I gave up time with friends. Time with family.

I alienated anyone who wasn't related to hockey until the only true friend to remain is my brother.

And honestly, I've been a dick to him too. He's only still around because he's my brother.

What am I supposed to do now? I have one good eye and the other one doesn't work at all. Scars decorate the left side of my face, which is still healing from a broken orbital bone. Not only did I lose my livelihood, but I'm damaged and ugly now too.

I never thought of myself as a vain person, but seeing those long scars? Not even being able to open my damn eyelid? I want to erase my entire face. Cover up. Hide from the disgusting jagged and puckered skin.

I'm a loser. I even have nightmares from the attack. Not that I remember anything other than terror when I wake up. I drown my sorrows with alcohol. Nothing changes, but at least the wounds numb instead of pulsating with pain.

I sit up as my door opens. Jenet stands in the doorway. It's unfortunate that I never asked for my key back after I let her have one when Jasper died. I don't even care she's here. My mind has been on the playoffs. The fucking playoffs! My stomach rolls with nausea at what I'm missing. Our conference final will wrap up tonight. Game seven. It's tempting to think about what I would be feeling if I was at the arena. It's easy to think about what I've lost. I'd rather not think at all.

Jenet walks slowly over to me as if I may detonate at any second. It's possible.

She sits next to me, grabs the remote, puts on *Lord of the Rings* since we've yet to watch the first movie entirely, and rests her head on my shoulder. I don't want her here. I guess I can tolerate her if she isn't going to talk.

After about thirty minutes, she pulls out her phone and takes a selfie of us.

"What the fuck are you doing?" I don't want my picture taken. The scars on my face are red and ugly. I wouldn't be surprised if children run away in fear if I ever leave the house and am spotted.

"Caroline needs proof of life."

I used to think Jenet was my weak spot. The thing in my life that made me do things I normally wouldn't for ridiculous reasons like to see her smile or to hear her laugh.

When in the hell did that become a six-year-old?

I don't even like the kid. I mean, she's okay, sure. She's all about sports like her dad wanted her to be. She likes to watch ridiculous cartoons. She's clingy. I'm sure that has to do with her father dying and then me getting hurt after that mini bonding session we had.

But she's not *my* problem.

Ugh.

Still.

"She okay?"

"She wants to see you and she's worried, but yes."

Hm. Not sure how I feel about any of that, so I do what I've been doing best. Pushing people away. "You don't have to be here."

She sighs. When it seems apparent she doesn't plan to respond, I'm compelled to continue.

"I don't want you here."

"Well, I want to be here and honestly, Cal, I need to sit here and feel you next to me after everything, so shut up so we can sit in peace."

There's nothing to say to that, so I stay quiet.

"We were both scared," Jenet adds.

Once again, that damn image of a sad Caroline sitting on my countertop comes to mind. The scream when she thought Jenet was going to make her leave the hospital echoes in my ears.

"Call her," I say before I can really think about it. I don't want to see her, or for her to see me, but there's no reason to be a real bastard and worry the kid.

Jenet hesitates. "Why don't you shower first? Sober up a little."

I sigh. That requires energy. Being sober doesn't sound nice either.

"She's really worried?" I ask. There's no reason to exert this effort if hearing from me won't make a difference.

"She's not convinced you won't disappear like Jasper because she can't see you," Jenet confirms.

Fuck. "I don't even like kids," I blurt out. Jenet tenses next to me. I keep going. "I never want kids. I'd be a piece of shit dad."

"Cal," Jenet starts, her voice all soft. "Go take a shower."

I don't understand why she's not upset, but whatever. I take my shower, sober up a bit with water and coffee, and sit silently next to Jenet. I want to feel like shit for what I said, but numbness overwhelms me.

After a bit, Jenet calls Carol who puts Caroline on the phone. Jenet hands it to me.

"Hey, kid."

"Cal! Mommy said you're home now."

"Yeah, I'm home." I've been home, but it doesn't sound like Jenet told Caroline that.

"Can I come see you?" she asks.

"Not yet. I'm still not feeling too great."

"Can you come to one of my games when you feel better?"

I want to do that about as much as I want to light myself on fire. Still, I say, "I absolutely will."

"Mommy sent me a picture." I wince and before I can respond, she says, "I'm sorry you have scars, but Daddy said scars make you tough and strong. Now, you're more strong. That's good."

This kid. "Thanks, Caroline. That makes me feel better," I lie. "Did you have school today?" I ask to get her talking about something else. After about fifteen minutes, I'm able to get her off the phone.

"Thank you," Jenet says softly.

"For what?"

"For putting her before yourself."

I bristle at that, but stay quiet. Maybe she'll leave me alone if I'm horrible company.

———

Three days pass. The Rebels are in the finals. What a hard fucking pill to swallow. It would've been easier to die than try to process the changes I must endure. To make things worse, Jenet is here again.

"She doesn't have many games left, Cal. You promised her you'd go and that's all I hear now. You *will* go because if you break a promise to my daughter, I'll break your legs."

At that, I can't help but chuckle. She thinks broken legs scare me? Not anymore. Still, the idea of letting Caroline down makes my skin crawl. Jenet warned me she would stop by to pick me up, so I somehow managed to be sober, showered, and dressed.

Now that the moment is here, I'm not too sure about this. I haven't left the house since my discharge. People will see my face. That's why Jenet's reading me the riot act. Because I'm hesitating. I'm thankful she didn't bring Caroline with her. Her grandparents have already headed to the ball field with Caroline.

"I'm nervous," I admit.

Jenet loops her arm through mine. "You can lean on me. It'll mean the world to Caroline," she reminds me. "Just one game."

I sigh. "I don't know how people tell either of you no."

Jenet beams a smile at me and off we go. The closer we get, the worse my anxiety is. All I can think about is how much I don't want to be here. My hesitation made us late, so the game is in full swing by the time we arrive.

That doesn't stop Caroline from spotting me. Apparently,

her eyes were peeled on the crowd because the relatively quiet atmosphere is suddenly disrupted by shouts of my name.

"Cal! Cal! Over here! Cal!"

I tug the baseball cap lower on my head, but walk over to the dugout.

"You came!" she exclaims as she claps her hands.

"Said I would." I tilt my head toward the bleachers. "I'm going to sit and watch."

"Can we get ice cream after the game?"

I laugh. I swear, her mind is always on ice cream. "Maybe."

Jenet tells her to focus and we make our way over to the bleachers to take a seat. Carol and Jacob, Jasper's parents, shake my hand and say hello, but otherwise dismiss me. Every moment that passes, I feel like more and more people stare at me.

I don't know if they are because I'm too chicken to look around. Still, it feels like dozens of eyes are on me and my stupid scars.

"I don't think I can do this," I say to Jenet as quietly as I can. Not quietly enough because Jasper's parents throw a glare my way.

Jenet squeezes my hand. "We just got here. Caroline would be devastated if you left so soon."

I take a deep breath and release the air slowly. T-ball is stupid and boring. Kids hit the ball off the tee. They run as fast as they can while five other kids scramble to get the ball and attempt to tag the hitter out.

The most ridiculous part is how the parents cheer. For *everything*. Miss the throw? Good try anyway! Can't hit the ball off the tee after three tries, go for a fourth. I'm being ridiculous, I know, but those are the thoughts filtering through my mind.

A commotion in the dugout drags everyone's attention

away from the field. Jenet stands and rushes over, leading me to believe Caroline is involved. Slowly, I follow after her. Just in case.

I scoff to myself. As if either of them would need me. What good am I anymore? I'm worthless now. My entire fucking life is absolutely worthless.

"What in the world?" one of the coaches asks as he separates Caroline and some punk-looking kid.

"He said my friend was scary and mean looking!" Caroline accuses. All the air leaves me as I realize they're talking about me. "He was *hurt*!" Her little chest inflates with her breath. *"You're* mean!" she snaps, pointing her finger at the kid.

For a second, I want to literally run away. Except…a weird warm feeling hits my chest as I realize this little kid thought she needed to defend me. *Me!* It's oddly sweet. Her defense of me somehow allows me to take what feels like the first breath of fresh air since the attack.

"Kid," I start before I even know what I'm doing. Caroline whirls around at the sound of my voice. She almost looks horrified that I overheard. I crook my finger and she closes the distance between us until only the fencing of the dugout separates us. I squat to be eye level with her. "It's okay if he thinks that. I *am* a little scary looking right now." She opens her mouth to protest, but I talk over her. "Think you can ignore him so I can see you play and use that killer arm your dad gave you?"

"It was mean," she points out, her brows furrowed.

Jenet crouches down next to me. "Honey, that doesn't mean you push him." Jenet takes over and within a minute, Caroline apologizes for pushing the boy and the game moves on.

"She likes you," Jenet tells me as we take our seats again.

"Not sure why," I answer honestly, but Jenet laughs as if I'm joking.

I manage to stay in the moment throughout the game and afterward as we get ice cream, Jenet asks me to stay, but I shake my head. Today was enough.

Later, I'm sitting at home with that blank TV screen when my mind wanders over to the looming final games of the season. The Rebels made it. Part of me is in a state of disbelief while the other half rages in protest. Fuck, why do I hate their success thus far so much? Why do I want to drown in liquor knowing this? Why couldn't I be on the ice too? Why did my life crumble faster than I could blink?

A lack of willpower has me grabbing a bottle of beer. I move over to the studio apartment to paint. Caroline's painting is finished and has long since been set aside. The hypnotizing blue of Jenet's eyes don't draw me in today. Instead, I grab a fresh canvas and all the colors.

Without thinking, without any effort, I let my hand lead. Throwing splashes of red, black, blue, and gray onto the canvas. The paint clashes against one another as I try my damnedest not to drown in the murky, thick, sticky black substance that increasingly covers my body and soul.

For a moment, a tiny flutter of what feels like bliss surges through me.

Finally. Everything is quiet. Blank. Void and numb in a non-suffocating way.

Maybe I'll drink and paint myself to death so I don't have to face the fact that my life is meaningless now.

# CHAPTER 13
## JENET

al continues to pull away. I thought we made a little breakthrough when he went to Caroline's game, but the final round starting sucked him back down. I check on him frequently, but he is lost.

He's so lost that even though he's physically right in front of me, I don't know if I'll ever be able to find him again. When I visit, he refuses to talk to me, though he'll sometimes call Caroline to relieve her of worry.

He's been drinking pretty heavily. I think the only time he eats is when I bring food over. It's clear how much he's spiraled out of control. Often, I find him in the studio apartment next door where he likes to paint. He never acknowledges me when I'm in the space with him. I'm not sure if it's because he doesn't want me there or because he doesn't realize I am there to begin with.

His paintings have turned dark too. More abstract and furious. I wish I can help him somewhat, but I'm clueless as to how.

Amongst all of that, I can't stop thinking about what he said about kids. It doesn't make sense to me. I've seen how fantastic Cal is with Caroline and she's not even his.

Why does he think he'll be terrible? Does he really not want kids? That certainly puts a wrinkle in the fact that we're together. Why would he stick around if he doesn't want kids? It's clear he understands with me comes Caroline.

I stop by Julie's after work one day before picking up Caroline.

"Jenet," Collin answers the door with surprise.

"Hey, sorry to drop by. Is Julie around?"

He nods and steps aside to let me inside. I find Julie in the kitchen.

"Jenet! Hey. How's Cal?"

"He's still ignoring us," Collin adds with a frown.

"Not great," I reply honestly. I focus on Julie. "You told me Cal had demons. What did you mean?" I hesitate and then ask, "Does it have anything to do with his art?"

Collin and Julie frown. "His art?" Collin asks. "What are you talking about?"

I shake my head as a weight rests on my chest. I knew I shouldn't have mentioned that. "What did you mean?" I repeat to Julie.

Collin and Julie exchange a glance.

"I don't think it should be us who tells you," Collin inputs.

Yeah, I'm not accepting that. There's no way I can question Cal right now. "I need to know. What if it could help me help him?" When that doesn't persuade them, I add, "He told me he never wants kids and would be a horrible dad. Is that related? Did you know he felt that way? Why would you set us up?"

Julie sighs and Collin must realize she's going to talk because he says, "Jules, it's not our place."

"She's right; this could help her help him."

Collin mutters under his breath and walks out of the room. Julie puts her full attention on me.

"Promise me that you'll listen to everything and not walk away."

"I can't promise that. I have my daughter to think about and you set me up with someone, let me allow him to get close to my daughter, and now you're confirming he doesn't even want kids!" This is unbelievable. I can't believe there's truth to all of this. The words do *not* match the actions.

Julie reaches over to rest a hand over mine. "Just remember all those good memories you have of Cal with your daughter. He told you we dated in high school, right?"

I nod and then listen as Julie recounts what happened after they broke up. How her period was late, she thought she might be pregnant, and Cal told her to have an abortion if she was.

"He was not as brave as your Jasper," Julie says. "Cal had a singular focus, didn't love me, and he made a rash decision. I thought he was a cold-hearted bastard, but turns out he always regretted it. Unfortunately, Cal is not good with regret. He couldn't force himself to find out what happened until I told him after I started dating Collin.

"Jenet, I had no idea this even affected him, but it's apparently ruled his life. All he cares about is hockey yet somewhere in his heart, he mourns the loss of a baby that never existed. Over his decision and lack of strength. With hockey gone, it wouldn't surprise me if he was drowning in regret and thinking the worst."

More to herself, she adds, "He's more like his brother than I gave him credit for." Julie sighs and refocuses on me. "Please tell me you won't walk away. Cal has been seeing someone to try and get over his guilt. Or he was before his injury. He's been a fantastic person with Caroline and, Jenet, he's not even like that with Wyatt because he looks so much like Collin and reminds him of what he did."

I don't say anything because I don't know what to say. This is a lot. On top of Cal feeling like his life falling apart and me trying to hold the pieces together, he apparently doesn't like or want kids because of a knee-jerk reaction that he's clung to as time's passed.

"Jenet, you two are perfect together. You really are," Julie says when I've been quiet for too long. "Don't hold this against him."

"I don't," I answer honestly. It would be unfair to hold this against Cal when I didn't know him then and it has nothing to do with me. People change and grow. I think Cal has, though he clearly doesn't agree. "I don't know how to help him."

Julie gives me a small smile. "Just don't give up on him. If you could convince him to at least answer Collin's calls, that would be nice."

I shake my head. "Sorry, but your husband is a living, breathing reminder of what Cal no longer has and no longer is. I'm not pushing that. Not right now at least."

Julie frowns, but nods in understanding. I thank her for sharing about Cal's past and then go on my way. Even more than usual, I want to see Cal, but I've already been at his house twice this week while Caroline had a sleepover with her grandparents.

Once I'm home, I send him a text.

JENET

I'm not going anywhere, Cal. We're here whenever you're ready. We miss you.

I get no response, not that I was expecting one. The only thing I can do is what I've done so far. Show up, spend time with him, feed him, and wait for his grieving to lessen enough that I can help him move forward.

———

Tonight, I can feel it in my bones that he needs me. The Carolina Rebels just won the Stanley Cup. Cal lived for hockey and this will send him spiraling even further, which I wouldn't think could be possible.

When I get to Cal's apartment, I take a deep breath and use the key to let myself in. Cal tolerates me at this point, but he refuses to have anything to do with Collin. Collin tries to talk to him and Cal loses his damn mind every time.

I've been doing my best to be here for Cal, to support him. I worry I'm inadvertently doing more harm than good. It hasn't been that long since his injury. I'm not expecting him to snap out of this anytime soon, but at the same time, he's spiraled so far, so damn fast.

He doesn't even speak to me anymore. He either stares off into space or is so caught up in his painting that it's become awkward to stick around. I push through, though. Cal was a pillar of strength for me and Caroline when Jasper died. Being here for him is the least I can do.

I quietly close the door behind me and easily spot Cal lying on the couch where I so often find him. I wonder if he's even been sleeping in his bed at this point. There are easily a dozen beer bottles on the coffee table.

"Go away, Jenet," he slurs without opening his eye.

My dumb heart beats faster with anticipation and relief that he's addressed me.

"I'm sorry."

In a move so fast I barely catch it, Cal sits up and flings his bottle across the room where it shatters upon impact with the wall. "I'm sick and tired of you coming over here and feeling sorry for me."

"So you're the only one who can pity you?"

He glares at me and my heart aches at the sight of his face. Cal doesn't say anything. He only stares at me, hoping I'll cower and leave.

"Leave, Jenet. No one asked you to be here," he finally snaps.

"Your life isn't over." When he scoffs at that, anger that has been simmering within me surges forward. "You're *alive*, Cal. You know who isn't? Jasper. Get the fuck over yourself! You can breathe and do whatever you want. Take advantage of it before no one is willing to help you."

He stares at me for a moment. "You don't understand."

"Then make me. Losing the game is hard, I know that, but you can find something new, Cal. Maybe your art."

He shakes his head, already looking defeated. "It was my life," he whispers. "The only goal I ever had. The only thing I ever wanted to do. The only thing I was *good* at. And now it's gone. I never had a plan B, Jenet. All my eggs were in this one basket. That basket is now in smithereens. What am I supposed to do now, Jenet?

"I never thought about retirement because it was too fucking scary to think I might not have the game. I stuck my head in the sand and pretended it would never happen. I wanted to play until I literally couldn't anymore. I sacrificed so much for it and it was for nothing. Nothing, Jenet. I have zero to show for it. It all means *nothing* now."

For a moment, I hesitate, but then I can't help but ask, "Is this about what happened with Julie when you two were in high school?"

Any softness disappears. He straightens until his back is ramrod straight and all his muscles tense. "How the fuck do you know about that?"

I fidget in my seat. "Julie told me. After what happened," I motion to his eye, "I pressured her to tell me because she once made a comment about demons you have. She thought I should know so I'd understand part of why you may be hurting."

"Get out." He nearly interrupts me for how fast he says it. His tone is eerily calm yet full of fury.

"Cal," I start to protest. He's never asked me to leave and if he is now, he may not let me come back.

"And leave the key when you go."

"Cal," I whisper. He can't do this. I can't walk out that door. I need to stay. I know it with every fiber of my being.

"I wish I died," he admits quietly. He remains still yet he appears to crumble before me. "I wish I died and Jasper didn't. I hate myself so much I can't stand it. I can't stand the idea of seeing my brother because it's like looking in a mirror. And now, he's out celebrating what should've been our fucking win and I can't stand it. How weak does it make me that a fucking *game* was my *life* and I don't want to live without it." He sighs and leans back, closing his eye. "Just go."

The defeat in his tone raises goose bumps on my arms. There's no way I can leave. Not when I know he wishes he was dead. I'm not sure how far the depths of his depression goes, but it's clear we're wading in dangerous waters.

With a deep breath to fortify my defenses, I grab his hand and pull him to stand. I take it as a positive sign that he doesn't immediately push me away and stands easily.

He sways on his feet and leans into me. I lead him to his bedroom. I'm not sure when he last showered, but showers always make me feel better, so I take us to his bathroom.

"What's the point?" he asks as I turn on the water and wait for it to warm up. When I glance over at him, my stomach bottoms out. He's serious. His gaze is clearer than I've seen it in a while and he seems expectant. As if he wants me to answer him. "What's. The. Fucking. *Point*, Jenet?" he repeats.

"Point of what?" I ask softly. I'm not sure I even want his answer.

"Taking care of myself. Eating. *Living*." His voice cracks with the last word.

I want to wrap my arms around him. Anchor him to this

world. To me. My heart shreds at knowing he's this lost and hopeless. So I do. I step closer and hug him as tight as I can as if that will bind him to me.

"*You* still matter, Cal. To a lot of people, even without the game. Your brother, Julie, Wyatt, and your parents care. I care. Caroline cares. I know you dedicated your life to hockey and things probably feel pretty empty without it, but we can find other things to fill the void. This day was always coming; it just came way sooner than you expected."

He nods, though I still don't like the look in his eye. I release him and watch as he sheds his clothes and steps into the shower.

"You don't have to be here." He says it softly, almost reluctantly.

I've never despised a single sentence so much in my life. He's said it to me at least once every visit. He puts up with me visiting, but at the same time, part of him wants to push me away for good. There's no urge to leave whatsoever. As much as I want to chain Cal to me, I already feel as if I'm chained to him.

I lean against the wall with a sigh. "You don't want me here?"

There's a long pause, so long that I don't think he plans to respond. But then he speaks so quietly I nearly miss it. "It's not that I don't want you here. I just…I don't deserve for you to be. I love you and Caroline, and I appreciate what you're doing, but you both deserve better."

My heart stutters at his casual declaration. With a deep breath, I say, "I love you too, so you should understand that I won't ever abandon you." I wait a beat to see if he'll respond. When he doesn't, I add, "I'm going to put clean sheets on the bed."

I leave him to his shower and check his sheets. They reek of alcohol, so I peel them off the bed and find clean ones to replace them.

When there's a soft knock on the door, I answer it.

"You can't be here," I reluctantly tell Collin when I see him. I literally just pulled Cal from the brink. It's sweet Collin wants to check on him after winning the Cup, but it's a horrible idea. The absolute worst. The last thing he needs is a reminder of what his life is not.

"Jenet," Collin starts. "He's refused to see me since the hospital. He's barely talked to me. I just need to make sure he's okay."

"Tonight isn't the night. He knows. He's not okay. And I don't think seeing you would be good for him."

A look of conflict crosses his features. "How bad off is he?"

"Go home to your wife and child, Collin," I answer, avoiding the question. "I'll be here with him." Without waiting for him to speak again, I close the door and lock it. With a sigh, I rest my forehead against the door. Hopefully, that was the right decision.

"Thank you."

With a screech, I whirl around to see Cal with only a towel wrapped around his waist. "You're not mad?"

He shakes his head. "Go get Caroline and then come back."

"Cal," I start.

"I miss her," he admits with a hint of surprise in his tone. "I know I haven't done right by her, or you. I know I've been a bastard to be around, but if you'll go get her, I'll behave," he promises. "I just…" Silence fills the room as he struggles with what to say. "I can't keep sitting here by myself. She's a little sunshine and I don't want to worry her anymore."

Part of me wants to turn him down because I'm not sure he's stable enough to expose my daughter to him. On the other hand, this is the first time he's asked to see her. This would do my daughter some god. This also seems like a good opportunity to…well, corner Cal into moving forward somewhat. With a breath, I say, "If I go get her, there's no more hiding away from us. This means you're all in. She lost her dad. I can't put her in a position where she'll get hurt again."

He nods. "I understand. I won't disappear on her again."

I want to believe him, I really do, but I don't trust his word just yet. Still, this is the first thing he's asked of me. Can I really deny him? "Why don't you come back with me instead?"

He immediately shakes his head. "Too much right now."

I hesitate for a moment, causing him to add, "Please?"

His please does me in every time.

"I will rip your arm off if you are mean to my daughter in any way."

Cal grins and I relax a little until it slides off his face. He seems a little nervous now, so I tell him to tidy his apartment the best he can, mainly the broken glass, and then I hurry out before he can change his mind. I work as quick as I can to drive home, pack a quick bag for Caroline, and then wake her to get her in the car.

Doing something like this is something I'd typically avoid, but if it'll help him...

And I know it'll do Caroline some good.

"Where are we going?" she asks groggily once we're in the car.

"To see Cal."

She immediately perks up. "Really?"

"Yeah, hun. He's excited to see you."

Anxiety boils in my stomach the closer I get to Cal's apartment. What if he's fallen back into the pit of despair since I left? Am I really making the right choice bringing Caroline over? It's only been like a month.

When I open the door to his apartment and see him in his pajamas, the room's tidy, and Caroline runs over to him, I relax. He kneels from where he stands in the kitchen with a bottle of water and lets her crash into him.

"Hey, kid," I hear him softly say. I wasn't too sure at first how I felt about him calling her kid, but I think it's a term of endearment for him. "Sorry I haven't been up for visitors, but it sure is good to see you."

"I missed you," she says as he picks her up and stands.

"Missed you too. I have a surprise for you. A present. If you like it and want to keep it."

Her eyes light up. Cal walks over to a canvas I didn't realize was sitting on the kitchen counter. With one hand, he tilts it up. His paintings and drawings are off limits to even speak about. For him to give one to Caroline? I have no idea how to feel.

"Is that me and Daddy?" she asks softly. Almost as if she knows how huge this moment is.

"Yeah."

I move closer and tears fall as I see how Cal ever so lightly painted angel wings on Jasper. Feather light and barely there, but glistening enough to catch your eye and show that he's an angel.

"Baseball was his favorite," she reminds him, all excited now. "And he has wings! Guarding angels have wings, right?"

"Right. When you're missing him or want to talk to him, you can look at this if you want."

"Thank you! Daddy would like it."

Cal manages a chuckle. "I'm glad."

When she yawns, he says, "Let's get some sleep." He heads down the hallway with her and I follow along.

"Can we go skating tomorrow, Cal?" she asks as she rests her head on his shoulder. "Mom hasn't taken me in a while."

I hold my breath, wishing I warned her not to talk about that. I should've been preparing her for this.

"Not quite up for that yet, kid," he tells her quietly. "But we'll get you back on the ice soon if you want."

We get settled in his bed much like that night when I

rushed over after learning of Jasper's death. This time, Caroline is in the middle of the two of us. We're all a little cuddled together.

"I'm glad you're okay," Caroline whispers. She wiggles closer to him and within a few minutes her breaths even out. I almost want to apologize. I don't want what she says to trigger him. Cal's hand finds mine; he gives it a squeeze and lifts it. A moment later, I feel him press a kiss to my knuckles.

"Night, Jenet."

"Night," I whisper back.

I can only hope this means he's on a path toward healing.

# CHAPTER 14
## CAL

'm not cured. I still hate my life. But with Caroline giggling over whatever cartoon I let her play on my TV, I don't feel nearly as dead inside as usual. There's a faint heartbeat pulsing somewhere deep down unfortunately. Jenet still sleeps, a sign that she's run herself raggedly lately between checking in on me, working, and taking care of her daughter.

I'm glad Jenet came. I'm not sure exactly what triggered me to request she bring Caroline over, but it's been weeks and I'm exhausted. I'm lonely. Such a weird thing to feel after all these years of not caring. I removed anything on my phone that could remind me of what I lost. The Rebels will be celebrating for a bit; I don't want to know about any of it. Keeping up with the team makes me hate myself more.

I almost felt bad about ignoring Collin, but I just can't yet. The relief I felt when Jenet sent him away without really telling him anything was proof of that.

"Cal?"

"Yeah, kid?" I ask, looking down to where Caroline sits next to me.

"Are you feeling better enough to come over again?"

What a loaded question. How do I answer that honestly? After a beat, I simply answer, "Maybe. We'll see."

"Does it hurt?" She props herself onto her knees and ever so gently touches one of my scars. If it was anyone else, I might've lost my shit. Caroline is just a curious, concerned kid. I can rein in my disgust and fury for her.

"Not anymore."

Caroline frowns. "So you are better?"

"Sometimes, you can't see where a person hurts."

She touches my closed eyelid and I flinch. I can't even see half of her fucking body unless I turn my head. My muscles are locked in place with her touching my face, so that's out of the question.

"I'm sorry! I didn't mean to hurt you. Why don't you open your eye?"

I take a slow, steady breath. "You didn't. I can't see your hand, so you surprised me." I frown as her brows shoot up. Did Jenet not tell her? "My eyelid and my eye don't work anymore."

Her little mouth falls open. Then a gleam appears in her eyes. "So you're like a pirate now?"

I laugh. Only because she's so excited at the prospect of me being like a pirate. "I guess so."

"Do you have an eyepatch? Pirates have eyepatches. And sometimes hooks for hands or a peg leg, but if you're a pirate now, you need an eyepatch."

"I don't, but maybe we can buy one."

"What about a blue one!" She claps her hands and I laugh again.

"They are supposed to be black, aren't they?"

Caroline rolls her eyes at me. "You can change it. Blue is my favorite color like Daddy's."

I nod seriously. "Blue then."

"Mommy! Cal is a pirate now and is going to wear a blue eyepatch! Isn't that cool?"

I'm forced to move, turning my head to see Jenet actually stands a few feet away. She opens her mouth, but I beat her to it.

"Hungry?"

"I overslept and we need to head out. Caroline, honey, go get dressed so I can take you to the sitter's."

The kid and I both frown at the same time. My chest didn't feel too tight until she mentioned leaving me here alone. While I don't want to face life head on any time soon, I do want to tread water just enough to be around Jenet.

And Caroline.

I'd never admit either of those things, though.

Caroline disappears into my bedroom without much argument.

"Will you do anything today?" Jenet asks with hesitation.

I shake my head.

"Maybe you should get out of the apartment."

I scoff. "I think I should stay hunkered down for at least another month." When she frowns, I add, "When you leave today, you're only going to see and hear about one thing."

The thing that I refuse to acknowledge or think about.

Jenet steps closer and cups my face with her hands. "You can't hide away here forever." I open my mouth to argue that I'm not, but Jenet doesn't give me the chance to protest. "Take all the time you need. I'll support you however I can. I still think you should push yourself to at least come over to my house, though." She kisses me before taking a step back, just as Caroline returns, dressed for the day.

She runs over and I crouch just in time for her to crash into me. "Bye, Cal! I love you; I'll miss you!"

My muscles tense, but Caroline is none the wiser. She releases me and races over to the door without waiting to see if I'll say it back. I'm too shocked, horrified, and terrified to speak.

Jenet squeezes my hand and quietly says, "Don't freak

out. You've earned what she said. You deserve it. I'll check in on you later."

And then they're gone. The silence and emptiness overwhelms me. My phone buzzes and I sigh when I see it's from Collin. I love my brother, I do, but he's driving me crazy. His texts lately are a bit much.

COLLIN

How are you today?

I'm here if you need anything.

Everything will be fine; I'm sure the team can find you a position if you want.

Will you please answer my calls? I just want to talk to you.

You're not alone.

How long will you avoid me? I'm your twin for god's sake.

I decide to finally respond to him.

CAL

Leave me the fuck alone, Collin. Just stop.

Okay, I probably could've been nicer, but I'm reaching my wits' end. Collin is everything I'm not now; forgive me if I don't want to see or talk to him. I hope I get there eventually, but right now? I'm struggling to even exist.

I spend most of my day in what's for all intents and purposes my studio. My paintings have turned a bit chaotic and abstract. I don't mind as long as the suffocating feeling purges in the meantime. The antsy feeling doesn't disperse. There's an itch to drink, but I keep thinking about what Jenet said. The promises I made to her. The promises about Caroline.

The chance to forget all of this and breathe easy sounds so

appealing, but how to make it happen? An idea forms and I make plans. Plans I hope Jenet will indulge me with. Plans that plant a tiny seed of hope in my chest.

That little seed spurs me forward as I pack and then leave my apartment. The idea of driving makes me nervous, so I order a ride instead. Jenet isn't home when I arrive, so I sit on the porch to wait. If she says no, I'll just go alone. At least, that's what I keep telling myself. We'll see. I hope I'm not faced with that prospect.

Some time later, Jenet pulls into her driveway. She throws me a beautiful, blinding smile. After she helps Caroline out, the little girl runs over to me.

"Cal! You're here! Do you want to throw the ball with me?"

Who knows if my vision is good enough for that even. "Maybe another time. I need to talk to your mom."

Jenet has unlocked the door at this point, so I add, "Why don't you go on inside?" When she opens her mouth to argue, I whisper, "I have a surprise, but I need your mom to say yes first. Go so I can convince her."

She nods and runs off.

"A surprise?" Jenet questions as she sits on the porch next to me. "Thank you for coming." She leans over and kisses my cheek.

"Do you have any plans this weekend?" When Jenet shakes her head, I continue, "Will you and Caroline come with me to the beach then?"

A look of disappointment flits across her features. "You can't run away, Cal."

I sigh. "I'm not. I just want two goddamn days where I can breathe and not be drowning in my apartment. Please, Jenet?" I grab her hand and interlace our fingers. "*Please*?" I beg again.

Relief floods me as she nods. "No more locking yourself away after this. I know you're going through an extremely hard time, but I don't want someone in and out of Caroline's life."

"Okay," I agree. It's not like I want to be miserable forever. I have zero hope that I'll find the level of happiness I had before, but there's no need to share that thought with Jenet.

"Did she say yes?" Caroline shouts from somewhere inside.

We both laugh and I stand, helping Jenet up. We head inside and I see Caroline on the couch, peering over the back at us.

"She said yes. Take your mom and pack your bags. We're going on a trip."

Her little eyes widen. "Where are we going?"

"To the beach."

She looks to Jenet who nods. Caroline hops off the couch and takes off running to her bedroom.

"Cal, how did you get here?"

"Ordered a ride. I've been cleared to drive, but…" I shake my head. She nods, kisses my cheek, and then disappears down the hall to pack.

Thirty minutes later, we're in the car, have stopped to grab something to eat, and are officially on our way to the coast. Caroline talks about her day and fills me in on all I've missed in her life. She falls asleep at some point.

The further we get from Raleigh, the easier I can breathe. The more I relax. This is exactly what I needed.

"Are you still talking to your therapist?" Jenet asks quietly.

And just like that, the uneasiness drowns me. "Did Julie and Collin just tell all my dirty secrets?" I snap as softly as I can; I don't want to wake Caroline. With a huff, I continue, "No, but I'll call next week. For the next two days, please don't mention anything about my life to me."

"Okay."

We eventually make it to the hotel and I carry Caroline

inside, resting her on the bed. My phone has been ringing nonstop for the past thirty minutes. Considering the only person I care to talk to is here, I've been ignoring it. But enough is fucking enough.

I pull it out to see Collin's name. A fury unlike anything I've ever felt toward my twin overtakes me. I step outside of the room to answer.

"What the fuck to do you want?" I snarl.

A whoosh of an exhale can be heard from the other end. "Thank god. I went over to check on you," my hand tightens on my phone at this, "and when you didn't tell me to fuck off, I got worried. Especially when I couldn't reach Jenet either. Where are you?"

"What part of leave me the fuck alone did you not understand, Collin?"

"Cal—"

"No, listen to me. My life is *ruined*. It's over, Collin."

"It's not—"

I ignore him and power on. "And you are literally the face of everything I lost and no longer have. I want some fucking space and the one time I need something from you, the *one time* I can't be the pillar of fucking strength you think I am and I need you to be it, you can't do the one fucking thing I ask?

"I was an asshole to you sometimes, I know, but if you needed something from me, I fucking did it, Collin. My entire life has been about catering to your needs and being there for you. For once, can you just return the fucking favor and leave me the hell alone?"

"No!" he snaps. "It's been long enough. You would've never let me wallow in misery like this. You would have jumped in to help pull me out. How can you expect me to sit on the sidelines and just let you flounder about? You won't see me or talk to me. You aren't talking to Mom or Dad. You aren't talking to anyone!"

"Long enough?" I scoff incredulously. "Sorry I'm not healing fast enough for you, especially when you just won the fucking Cup yesterday! And I talk to Jenet," I argue, but he cuts me off.

"No, you don't! You allow her to be around you, but you don't talk to her. I'm your twin for fuck's sake; you can't close me out. And your life isn't over. If you'd talk to me, you'd know that the team wants you there for the parade and they want to put your name on the Cup. You don't have to shut us out."

Something in me snaps. "You're fucking joking, right? I don't want a goddamn thing to do with the Rebels. I don't want to be in the parade and I certainly don't want my name on a trophy I didn't fucking win!" I shout. "If I want to leave town and never look back, I'll do it. I can do whatever the fuck I want, Collin.

"Why are you even pestering me? You finally got your wish. You'll be the better Kessy now. You always have been but you were too blind to see it. It's clear as day now who's superior; you shouldn't have the urge to compete with me anymore. You win. Now back the fuck off and give me my goddamn space!" I erupt.

My phone is pulled from my ear and I blink away the red haze to see Jenet.

"Go inside. I'll talk to him before you wake up everyone in the hotel."

Fine. She can deal with him. I escape into the hotel room, but lean against the wall just inside to listen to Jenet's side of the conversation.

"Hey, Collin," she says. "Can you please just leave him be? He'll come around when he's ready. He's okay. We're at the beach for the weekend, okay?"

She pauses and then she says, "He needs to handle this his own way, Collin. I know you're worried and upset he isn't leaning on you, but pushing him isn't helping. He has someone in his corner and that should reassure you. I won't let your brother get lost to this, I promise." Another pause. "He'll reach out when he's ready," she states more firmly. "Okay, thanks. Bye."

I step away from the door as she walks inside a moment later. She sighs when she sees me.

"Did you bring the thing I can't ask you about?"

Against my wishes, my lips fight a smile. "Yes."

"Get it then."

Even she can tell that the buzzing energy boils beneath the surface, just waiting to pull me under and drown me. I grab the sketchpad and follow Jenet out to the balcony. The salt air soothes my soul as I sit in one of the chairs and then pull Jenet to sit in my lap.

The world hasn't fallen apart with her knowledge of one of my actual deepest secrets. Besides, I want her close. I rest the pad of paper in her lap and let my mind and hand take over. Jenet rests her head on my shoulder and watches.

This…this right here is the very definition of peace. This is something I'll fight to have.

# CHAPTER 15
## JENET

The random lines slowly transform. My breath catches as I realize he's drawing Caroline and me. We stand next to one another and hold hands. Caroline looks up to me, but he hasn't completed her expression yet.

The only sound has been the scrape of the pencil over the paper and the ocean. The relaxing push and pull as the waves crash to shore helps erase the tension from his muscles with every stroke of the pencil. Normally, I try not to intervene when it comes to Cal and Collin, but Cal was irate, shouting, and that defeats the entire purpose of our time here.

When Cal speaks and shares details about his life without prompt, I'm completely caught off guard. I try not to even breathe because I don't want him to realize this isn't a dream and spook him.

"When Collin and I were growing up, it felt like everyone in our lives took the identical thing seriously. And then at some point, Collin's anxiety started and we started being treated differently. Which is why Collin thinks I'm the better Kessy even though I'm not.

"My dad in particular is probably the culprit. He got us involved in hockey and the moment he thought we could be great, things changed. He really focused on cultivating our love for the game and our skill. He wanted us to love it and excel at it.

"But at the same time, I had to look after Collin. Be there when he needed me. Be stronger than him for when he was weak, so I could be strong enough for us both. My role was to be everything Collin wasn't at times so he could lean on me and I could get him through it.

"So thanks to my dad, Collin put us both on these super high fucking pedestals. He was hard on himself when he failed his expectations and it was like I couldn't ever make a mistake because that didn't fit in either."

His voice lowers and there's a slight tremble in his hand. "Sometimes, I wonder if that's why I walked away from Julie, aside from the fact I was terrified and my dad agreed it was the right decision."

"Wait, what?" I can't help but interrupt. His dad knew and also thought he was in the right to tell Julie all that he did?

A soft sigh leaves Cal. "Yeah. I called my dad as soon as I hung up with Julie and explained what happened. I immediately regretted what I did and thought I should go over there, but Dad agreed it would be better to cut myself off completely from her so she wouldn't get in my or Collin's way. Any time I thought about reaching out to her, it's like Dad knew and would call me, reiterating what a bullet I dodged."

I can't even process this right now. Collin continues anyway.

"But I thought—and hoped—she would run to Collin and he'd see I'm not infallible. He'd see I was human. When she didn't reach out to him, I hated her even more and started drowning in my own self-hatred too."

He takes a deep breath. "Anyway, this—" He taps his hand on the paper. "This is something my dad never approved of. He was horrified. Told me enjoying this made me a pussy and weak. I think he just didn't like that I had an interest outside of hockey. He didn't want anything to take me away from that or being glued to Collin's hip.

"I buried it and abandoned it for a while but at some point, hockey wasn't enough of an outlet for me. I picked it back up, but kept it secret from everyone, even Collin. I didn't need my dad breathing down my neck over this."

After a few beats of silence, I glance up at him. His focus is still on his drawing. Just when I think he is done sharing, his low voice speaks again.

"Why weren't you upset over what happened with Julie? I clearly was not as good of a person as Jasper was."

"I have no business judging teenage Cal," I reply gently.

The pencil stops moving, but he doesn't lift his gaze to mine. "Don't you distrust me now? Aren't you worried about Caroline getting hurt? Or that I'll do the same if something similar happens in the future?"

Instead of answering, I say, "Tell me what you think about Caroline. How you feel about her."

His brows furrow, but he says, "She's a great kid. I'm glad I didn't let my gut reaction win and walk away after our first date because I'd probably be doing worse right now. She's a ball of sunshine." Cal frowns. "It worries me that she likes me so much, honestly."

"Because it makes you nervous for some reason or because you don't think you deserve it?"

Finally, his eye flicks to mine. "We both know I don't deserve it."

I take his sketchpad and pencil, setting them on the nearby table. Once I straddle his lap, I cup his face. He flinches as my fingers graze his scars. "You do. You play with her. You make sure she's okay. You ease her worries and fears. You've yet to let her down, even when you don't feel like doing something. Don't dismiss her love for you just because it scares you."

Cal lets my words soak in for only a moment before he grabs my wrists and pulls them away from his face. "We should go to bed; she'll be up early."

My shoulders slump at his dismissal. "Thank you for sharing."

"Thank you for not leaving," he nearly whispers.

———

The next day, we find ourselves on the beach. Cal and I help Caroline build a sand castle. This is probably the most relaxed and carefree I've seen Cal in...ever. Even when his life was going the way he wanted, he didn't seem as...free...as he does now. His injury may be a weird blessing in disguise—not that I'd ever say that to him.

Caroline keeps stealing glances at Cal. It's almost like she wants to say something. But then she focuses on me and she finally speaks.

"Is Cal my new daddy now?"

Cal freezes and I blink a few times. "What...why would you ask that?" I do my best to sound curious.

"Well, Frankie said his mommy starting hanging out with a boy a lot and now that's his new daddy."

"Your dad will always be your dad, Caroline," Cal interjects before I can. "I'm just...I'm just your Cal."

Inside, I want to beam at the fact he even answered her.

"Frankie didn't get a new daddy. His mommy and daddy don't live together anymore and his mommy got married to someone else. He has a stepdad." I can see the question on her face, so I add, "He just has someone else around to be there for him when his daddy can't be."

Caroline mulls on this for a bit but doesn't ask any more

questions, thankfully. It takes Cal about fifteen minutes before he relaxes again.

We spend the day in the sand or in the water. It's probably the most fun we've had in a while. It was definitely a good choice to come here. Later, after shower and dinner, Cal takes us to play putt putt.

"Am I winning?" Caroline asks after the fourth hole.

Cal nods without even checking with me, since I'm technically keeping score. "And your mom is last," he adds with a little laugh. "Maybe you should talk her through what you're doing so she can learn how to be better."

Okay, he's got me there. I didn't realize it was possible to be so bad at putt putt, but my skill level is nonexistent. And yes, my six-year-old is better at the stupid game than I am.

Caroline gives me a look and then nods. She takes Cal's advice because she says, "Okay, Mommy, so I stand like this." She jumps into her stance which is nothing special, but apparently, there's something to it. "And I close my eyes and I whisper, 'Daddy, please help me,' because Daddy took me to play putt putt before and he was *really* good." My eyes prickle at this. I thought she was whispering something, but I wasn't sure. "And then I do my wiggle." She wiggles her entire body and swings the putter as she says, "And hit the ball."

We watch as the ball climbs and then descends the hill, hits the little wall, and curves to fall perfectly in the hole.

Caroline squeals and Cal claps.

"Great job, kid. A hole in one! That's really good." Cal holds his hand out and Caroline runs over to complete the high-five.

"Mommy, did you see that?"

"I did! That was awesome."

"Okay, you try. Do what I did. Do you need me to show you again?"

Cal snickers, earning him a glare from me. "No, hon. I was paying attention." I do exactly as my daughter did. They both laugh when I wiggle and even harder when my ball doesn't even make it up the hill.

"Maybe I'm bad because I don't have good cheerleaders."

Cal barks out a laugh as he steps over to brush a kiss to my temple. "I think it's more like you're just bad. Sorry, Jenet."

For a moment, I freeze. This is the first display of affection from Cal in front of Caroline. Even sharing a hotel room together, he's woken me up so I can crawl in next to Caroline before she wakes up. And after her question this morning about a new daddy, I'm a little apprehensive in general.

Neither Cal nor Caroline mind me, and Caroline doesn't seem particularly interested in what Cal just did.

"Sorry, Mommy. I tried." She throws her hands up and shakes her head as my next stroke is a bit too hard, nearly causing the ball to return back to me after going over the hill and bouncing off the wall.

Cal and Caroline chum it up. They poke fun at me and give me so-called tips. Afterward, even though Cal won, he tells Caroline she did. She beams up at him like he just handed her the world. I really, really hope Cal doesn't let us down because it is clear my little girl likes him.

"Oh my goodness. Cal! Look!" Caroline squeals when we re-enter the building to return our putters. She runs across the room and jumps in hopes of reaching some item on a display rack.

Horror courses through me when I realize it's a blue eyepatch. The putt putt course is pirate themed and they have various colors of eyepatches for sale apparently.

"Obviously we need it," Cal replies without missing a beat. He grabs one and toss it onto the counter.

"Can I have one too?"

"Sure. What color?"

"Blue!"

He grabs another one and then looks at me. "You want one too?"

Oh my god. Is he seriously teasing me right now? He tone certainly suggests it. All I can do is shake my head. He smirks. Smirks! After he pays for the eyepatches, both he and my daughter proudly wear them.

"Well?" he asks her.

She throws a thumbs-up his way and then asks about ice cream. I'm not sure what happened to Cal, but this trip has certainly loosened him up.

———

The weekend is wonderful and relaxing. I'm not sure who has more fun, Caroline or Cal. We've only been home a few minutes before Cal takes my hand and squeezes it. He still wears that ridiculous eyepatch because Caroline said he should. That's it. That's literally the reason.

"I'm heading home."

My stomach sinks at Cal's declaration. He gives me an easy smile, though.

"You're right. I can't run, but I can't lean on you and Caroline as a crutch either. I'll be back," he promises. "And soon. I remember what you said about Caroline."

"Are you sure?"

Part of me feels as if this should be a proud moment, but on the other hand, I'm worried he'll spiral again.

Cal nods. He steps forward, hugs and kisses me softly, and then steps back.

"Hey, kid," he calls out. Caroline rushes back into the living room. "I'm heading home."

She pouts much like I feel like doing at the moment, but she doesn't protest. She hurries over to give him a hug.

"Are you coming back soon?" she asks.

"Yeah, I'll be back. I left you a surprise in your bag."

Her eyes widen, she shouts a thanks, and then rushes off to her room. Cal chuckles to himself, kisses me quickly again, and then he's gone. I watch as he gets into a waiting car outside.

"Mommy!" Caroline shouts as she runs back into the room, dragging my attention back to her. "Look!"

She waves a piece of paper in the air and then holds it out for me.

"Now I have one of you and me like me and daddy!"

My breath catches in my chest. It's the drawing Cal started at the beach. When did he even finish it? It's so realistic. Caroline holds my hand, looking up at me with a look of such adoration that mirrors mine.

"It's beautiful," I manage to say.

"Will you help me hang it?"

"Of course."

I get busy helping her and unpacking to settle back in and get ready for the next week. I can't help but feel as if my house is a bit emptier without Cal here.

# CHAPTER 16

## CAL

y apartment is a form of hell. The air is toxic and suffocating. I talk to Jenet and Caroline every night, but haven't managed to leave in a week. Sleep has eluded me, too. I paint, draw, or stare at my blank TV screen. It's been a week of attempting to purge these feelings and thoughts in my paintings. A week of wishing I wasn't here on this earth at all. I can't take it anymore.

A knock of my door causes me to stand and walk over.

"Collin will be so upset with me," Julie says from the other side.

"You're just helping," I reply, grabbing two bags and handing them to her before I pick up a box.

"Yeah, but you should've called him instead."

"I don't want to see him yet."

Julie looks like she wants to argue, but she wisely doesn't.

"Are you still going to the wedding?"

My shoulders fall just a bit. I'd already forgotten. Brayden and Deanna are getting married in a few weeks. I really, really don't want to go. I shrug and Julie leaves it at that.

We silently take a couple trips to her SUV. All my hockey stuff mocked me. I couldn't take it anymore. I needed it gone.

My brother's is the best place for it because throwing it away completely wasn't something I could do either.

"He misses you," Julie says softly once all the items are loaded in her vehicle. "Especially now that's it's summer. He doesn't know what to do with himself without you around."

"He'll figure it out. He's gotta adjust just like I do. After all, we don't work together anymore." My chest squeezes at that thought. My heart mourns the idea for us both. For better or worse, we've always been by each other's side. I'm not sure what either of us will do now that our paths are clearly diverging.

Julie frowns. "I think you both could figure it out better together."

"Julie," I sigh. "Please don't. I'll make it over at some point this summer. That's the best I can promise right now."

She nods. "I'll let him know you're okay."

"Thanks."

She gives me a quick hug and then goes on her way, thankfully.

I was hoping my apartment would feel lighter with all my stuff gone, but it's just as empty as before. For nearly three hours, I pace around, agitated and about ready to literally pull my hair out. Fuck this. I can't take this.

The apartment is like a black hole and I'm floating around without any way out. I'll shower and go to Jenet's. Keep my promise to her like I said I would.

I step out of the shower and hear voices coming from the living room. The fuck? I hurry to dress and then find Jenet and my father facing off.

"Dad? What are you doing here?"

He turns toward me and I stop in place at the look of utter disgust on his face. I know that look. I got it all the time as a kid whenever Collin wasn't around and Dad wanted to get on my case about something. My entire body stills and I brace.

"What the fuck are *you* doing, Cal? Ignoring your family and holing up in your apartment like a wuss. It's time to get the fuck over it. We'll figure something out. You can do something with the team, I'm sure, so you can stay close with Collin. We—"

"Sorry, Dad," I interrupt. "But in case you're also half-blind, Collin doesn't need me." And he doesn't. Whatever dependency he had on me became nearly nonexistent once Julie was fully in the picture. "I'm done with hockey." Even saying the word makes me want to vomit.

My dad scoffs. "And what do you think you'll do without it? Nothing. All your skills are tied up in the sport. You'd be worthless without it, Cal." Jenet releases a small gasp, but it's otherwise as if she's not here. "Get your life together and reach out to the team. You have two days before I come back and drag you out. I didn't raise a pussy. You understand me, Cal? You will get your shit together and you will not abandon your brother. I didn't spend all that time and money to help get you to where you were for you to let some fuckers work over your face and take the game away. Your brother still needs you and you'll step up to continue being there for him like you were raised."

Of course. Everything is about Collin and my supposed role in his life. Dad doesn't see the truth and it's that I'm already worthless without the game because it's over and I'm never going back in any capacity. Collin doesn't need me. He never has. Have I been helpful? Yes. But Collin doesn't *need* me, especially now. In actuality, at some point, *I* started to need Collin.

I mean for fuck's sake, he's literally my only friend; I'm honestly not sure he would even put up with me if not for being my brother. I tried to make an actual effort to get close to others, and Zane was the closest I got. Even then, our connection was hockey. And again, he got a woman and he'd rather be with her than put up with me. I've only heard from him three times since my injury, one of those being yesterday. Not that I blame him. The playoffs took a lot of their focus. I didn't respond to any of his texts either.

Why bother? I have nothing without the game, especially my brother. I'll probably lose him because hockey was what ultimately tied us together. Leave it to my father to point out the cold hard facts I've been trying to avoid. I have no one and my life means nothing now.

"You're such a bastard," Jenet comments, her tone one of disbelief.

Dad sighs. "Can you please get your puck bunny out of here? I'm surprised you still have one hanging around considering you can't play."

Jenet looks at me. She's probably wondering why I haven't kicked him out yet. What's the point? He'd just wait for her to leave and come back.

"You need to go," she tells him when I don't acknowledge her glance.

Dad shrugs, but gives me a pointed look. "Two days, Cal."

The moment he turns and walks out of my apartment, I turn and punch the nearest wall until a gaping hole is all that remains. Son of a bitch! I should've known that he'd come up here with me ignoring everyone and how he clearly can't accept the fact that Collin is a big boy who can take care of himself.

The last thing I want is him breathing down my neck. Reminding me at every corner how worthless I am if I don't follow the path he puts in front of me. I didn't have a problem with the path growing up, but now? I can't do it. I fucking *can't.* And if I don't do what he wants...

"Cal?" Jenet starts softly.

"Please go." She's normally a tiny reprieve that helps me keep her close for as long as she'll let me, but right now, her very presence suffocates me as much as the fact that my father is in town.

"Are you sure? I—"

"I'm positive." I lean my forehead against the wall. I don't trust myself to look at her and keep what barely remains of my sanity intact.

When there's only silence, I add, "I'll call you tomorrow. I promise. I'll even come over." How I'll manage that with how I currently feel, I'm not sure, but if it'll get her to leave, then I guess I'll try.

"Will you call me if it gets to be too much?"

I nod. "Promise," I swear.

She walks over and I tense as she stands behind me and wraps her arms around me. I wait out her hug. The soft kiss she places on my spine nearly undoes me.

"You promise?" she whispers, apparently needing me to double confirm.

Something about her tone makes me confess, "You and Caroline are the last thread holding together my sanity. I promise."

She squeezes her arms around me once and then does as I asked and leaves.

My dad's words play over and over in my mind as I grab the bottle of liquor I've been actively avoiding all week and return to my bed. Jenet made a comment before that my art may be an option. Briefly, I wondered too, but my dad just confirmed that's the coward's way out. For fuck's sake, let's not give him a pussy for a son.

And that's what I would be. In his eyes and maybe even in Collin's. Part of me hoped Collin would be an ally once I managed to pull myself out of the suffocating waters, but now I'm not so sure. Dad treats us differently and it wouldn't surprise me if he talked to Collin in such a way to think that he would need to convince me to find a path within hockey again just so we could stick close together.

Would I be worthless without my twin too? Is being Collin's sidekick and playing hockey what makes life worth living? Both of those are gone now. Hell, playing hockey might've been the only reason Collin kept me around; now that he has Julie? He doesn't need me. Not only because he has her, but also because he's strong enough to handle his own life.

If I can't play and if Collin doesn't need me…what the fuck am I even doing?

The alcohol burns down my throat as I guzzle it down. Down and down. How much alcohol until it kills me? Wonder if I have enough for that. One can hope. The depression that's coated my insides like a sticky tar can be replaced by the soothing liquid instead. How much would I need to drink for that to happen? For my dad to back the fuck off? Would he ever? Will he always breathe down my neck about hockey? Or will he eventually give up and then leer at me with disgust like he did when I walked into the living room and he saw my face?

I'm in a lose-lose situation. There's no light at the end of this tunnel. There's only darkness. Hell, the end of the tunnel doesn't even exist. The exit is barricaded with no way out. I'm doomed. That's the only truth I'm left with.

Right?

Jenet comes to mind first. And then Caroline. They could be my light until I claw my way out of the depths of the tunnel.

I sit up and nearly topple back over.

*Jenet. I need Jenet.*

I stand and manage to find my keys.

*Jenet. I need Jenet.*

My body bumps into walls as I stagger out of my apartment building.

*Jenet. I need Jenet.*

Maybe she can save me. And if not?

She's better off without me anyway.

# CHAPTER 17
## JENET

only intended to drop off dinner. I had just set the bag of food on the counter when there was knock at the door. A man barged in as soon as I opened it, looking for Cal. The rest that transpired blew my mind.

I thought my family could be bastards, but they have nothing on Mr. Kessy. It takes every ounce of willpower to actually leave Cal's apartment like he asked. Instead of picking up Caroline, I drive over to Collin's first.

Julie answers the door and I politely request to see her husband. She ushers me inside and calls Collin down.

"How could you let him go over there and talk to Cal that way?" I blurt out, still outraged on Cal's behalf.

Confusion filters over his face. "Who?"

"Your father."

"My dad's in town?" Collin repeats. "Jenet, start over. What's going on?"

As I rehash the entire conversation, the shock on their faces would be hilarious if not for the reason why. It's clear they never knew about this side of Cal's relationship with his father.

"He wouldn't let me stay. Will you go over in a bit and

check on him? Like you were just being your usual self wanting to see him and let me know how he is?"

Collin nods. "Yeah, sure. I had no idea Dad put that kind of pressure on Cal." He shakes his head, upset. "I can't believe he wants to push him toward the team when Cal is against it. I'll go see Cal and then I'll call my dad," he promises.

"Thanks."

I say my goodbyes and force myself to pick Caroline up from the sitter and head home when every instinct within me shouts to go back to Cal's.

"Mommy, can we go see Cal?" she asks the moment we step inside the house.

I don't think Cal realizes just how much my daughter has fallen in love with him. Not seeing him or talking to him as much as before the injury has confused her, though she knows he's still healing. She wants him to heal here with us and doesn't understand why he can't. Part of me thinks she's still worried he'll die like her dad. Or at the very least, that he'll disappear without regular contact.

"Not today, honey. Cal isn't feeling too good, but we can call him tomorrow to check on him, okay?"

She nods and runs off to her room to play. A horrible nagging feeling that has pestered my gut since I left Cal's weighs on me heavily. More and more with each passing moment. So much so that I want to text Julie to see if Collin has gone to check on Cal yet, but I don't. Not yet.

Some time later, my phone rings and I breathe out a sigh when I see Collin's name.

"How is he?" I answer.

"Jenet," Collin starts and his tone sets me on high alert. It's sad. Worried. It tells me that something is clearly wrong. "Julie is on her way over to your house right now, okay?"

"What's wrong?" I demand, tears already falling. My

heart races in my chest and I press my hand on my chest as if it'll slow it down.

"We're at the hospital."

Oh god. "Just spit it out, Collin," I snap.

"He was driving drunk and drove straight into a patch of trees not too far from your place. They're concerned about alcohol poisoning and he's hurt pretty bad. They…the officer said…he said there weren't any signs he tried to stop and it doesn't even look like he lost control."

Oh god. "They think he wrecked on purpose?"

"Maybe," Collin nearly whispers. "He's in surgery right now."

I squeeze my eyes closed. What am I going to tell Caroline? This will terrify her, especially if he's hurt worst than last time.

"Julie should be there any minute," Collin continues. "She can drive you here or if you'd rather she watch Caroline, she can take her to our place."

I thank Collin and then disconnect the call. With a deep breath, I swipe my tears away and walk back to Caroline's room.

"Hey, honey. Would you want to have a sleepover with Julie and Wyatt?"

She squeals in excitement and runs to her closet to pull out her bag. By the time I have her packed, Julie knocks on the door.

"Caroline is very excited. Thanks for offering to let her have a sleepover."

Julie nods. She looks like she wants to say something, but decides against it. I give my daughter a hug and see them off. The moment they disappear around the corner, I hurry to grab my things and rush to the hospital.

The moment I see Collin in the waiting room, I break down. He envelops me in a hug, but I wish it was Cal.

"He'll be okay," he promises.

"I should have stayed." I should have trusted my gut and not left him, especially after that episode with his father.

"You couldn't have known."

But I *suspected*. I *could've* known. Collin ushers me to a seat and lets me lean on him while we wait and wait and wait. It's well into the night, nearly morning, before a doctor comes out. All I manage to understand is Cal is now stable, but remains under sedation.

Another hour passes before we're allowed in his room. My breath catches as I finally lay eyes on him. One calf is in a cast. One of his forearms is in a cast. There are tiny scrapes all over his face and I'm sure there are some bandages or scars I can't see.

"Do you want to head home for a bit?" Collin asks.

I shake my head. I don't think I can ever leave his side again. After taking a seat in the chair next to his bed, I gently take his hand in mine.

"I'm going to call my dad; I'll just be right outside."

I nod, but I can't manage to take my eyes off Cal. Right before he steps out of the room, I come to my senses and say, "He's not allowed here."

If Collin wants to object, he keeps it to himself. The door clicks closed a moment later.

Did he wreck on purpose? Or was he so intoxicated that he wrecked? What was going through his mind? Has he given up? I sit next to his bed and wait for him to wake up. What am I supposed to say when he does?

My body is stuck in the chair as I wait. Late the next day, Collin convinces me to go home for a shower. We've been in the hospital for nearly twenty-four hours. I need to make a decision on if I'll let Collin stay with him tonight or if I'll make arrangements for Caroline so I can stay. My gut insists that I stay with him. My heart aches at the thought of leaving long enough to shower. How can I manage to be gone the entire night?

Once home and the droplets of water pelt down on me, I sink to the floor, wrap my arms around my knees, and cry. What if I lost him? How could he be so reckless? I know his mind is in a dark place, and I need to give him a lot of grace. At the same time, I want to be so incredibly selfish and find a way to snap him out of the darkness. For my sake. For Caroline's sake. For *his* sake.

Numbly, I manage to finish my shower and return to the hospital after a quick call to Caroline, who makes my decision easy by begging to spend the night with Julie and Wyatt again.

My heart beats erratically in my chest as my footsteps echo throughout the hallway. Each steps brings me closer to Cal's room and the anchor of anxiety in my belly gets heavier and heavier.

I pause when I push open the door to see Cal awake. His gaze clashes with mine and one of his hands balls into a fist. Is he upset that I'm here?

"Maybe you can get him to talk. I'll run home quick and come back with some dinner. Did you eat yet?" Collin asks me.

I shake my head.

He says something else, but my face burns and my hearing seems to have stopped picking up anything. Collin brushes past me a minute later and I finally step into the room, letting the door close behind me.

Cal holds out the hand of his good arm. I rush over, sit on the edge of the bed, and before I can worry if my hug will crush him, he wraps both of his arms around me so tightly, my lungs struggle to function. He grunts in obvious pain, but when I try to wiggle away, his hold only tightens.

"I'm sorry," he whispers into my neck. "I'm so fucking sorry, Jenet." And then he does the one thing I never expected him to do. He breaks down crying on my shoulder.

"Please don't ever terrify me like that again." My voice cracks and my tears begin to fall as well.

Cal squeezes me tighter. Part of me wants to ask if he wrecked on purpose, but part of me is petrified to hear his answer. I don't know if I can bear to hear the truth. We hold each other and at some point, the tears subside, but he doesn't release me.

"I'll get help," he whispers. "Please don't leave me."

I turn my face toward his neck and press a kiss there. "Never."

Cal loosens his grip, so I lean back to look at him. He wipes my tears and I nearly break down again at the pure anguish on his face. "What...does Caroline know I'm here?"

I shake my head.

"Can you not tell her? I don't want to worry her."

"Okay."

He rests his forehead against mine and sighs wearily. "They said I'll get discharged tomorrow. Can I stay with you for a bit?"

I agree without hesitation. If he's at my house, I can keep an eye on him.

"Lay with me."

"Cal—"

"Please."

With hisses of pain, he scoots over despite my protests. I carefully place myself next to him and rest my head on his shoulder.

"I love you," he whispers. "Just...don't leave."

"I won't."

————

The next evening, within minutes of us arriving at my house, there's a knock on the door. I open it and smile gratefully at

Julie. Caroline runs past me and squeals when she sees Cal. Her squeal is cut off by her gasp.

"Cal! You're hurt!"

I turn and watch her climb onto his lap. She throws her arms around his neck. I want to warn her to be careful since he has bruised ribs, but my words are stuck in my throat as I watch him hug her in return.

"Hey, kid," he says softly. "I'm okay. Got in a little car accident."

I'd snort if I could. He doesn't even have a car anymore. Caroline must ask him something, but I don't hear her since her face is buried in his neck.

Cal's good arm moves up and down as he rubs her back. "Yeah, your mom said I could stay here for a while." A pause and then, "I won't ever go away again, I promise." Another pause and finally, "Yeah, I'm really okay."

Swiping a tear, I turn to face Julie. She gives me a soft smile.

"Do y'all need anything?"

I shake my head. "No; thanks, though."

She gives me a quick hug and then she's gone. I take a seat next to them on the couch. Cal immediately moves a hand over to my thigh, as if not touching me means we'll disappear, never to be found again.

His face is creased with pain from Caroline snuggled against him.

"Caroline, honey, come sit in my lap instead. Cal's body hurts right now, okay?" The moment she nods, I reach over to lift her onto my lap, hearing the soft exhale from Cal.

I find Caroline's favorite cartoon and we watch that until it's time for bed. When I mention bedtime, she looks over at Cal.

"Will you read me a story, Cal?"

"Sure thing, kid."

I help him stand and he uses a crutch to wobble down to

her bedroom. I give them space, feeling as if they both need it. But I need to do something, so I grab my laptop and start catching up on some emails and rearranging my schedule from taking the last two days off work.

Thankfully, I didn't have anything pressing this week and a simple explanation that there was a family emergency soothed any protests from my clients.

At some point, I realize it's been some time and Cal should be back by now. I stand and quietly pad my way down the hallway. I peek into Caroline's room and my heart nearly stalls out.

Cal sits on the floor, his back against the side of her bed. A book rests against his thighs. His head is craned backward on the mattress, his eyes closed. There's no way he's comfortable. Or not in pain. How did he even get down there without being in pain? I enter her room and crouch next to him, carefully picking the book up and storing it away.

When I turn around, his eyes are on me. I hold out my hand and help him up. All he does is grit his teeth, though it must hurt like hell. I help him to my room and we change before attempting to get comfortable in my bed.

I can't take the unknown anymore.

"Did you purposely do it?" I whisper into the darkness.

Silence engulfs the room. To the point that surely the only thing either of us can hear is my heart hammering in my chest.

"The drinking, yes. Getting in my car, unfortunately. But I don't remember the entire trip. Maybe I did. Maybe I passed out. I don't remember; either is possible. My head was not in the best place. I'm sorry."

Still, I don't know. It sounds like neither does Cal. I'm not sure if that's a good thing or not. Before I can speak, Cal does.

"I left a voicemail at the therapist's office to set up an appointment." At this, I turn my head toward him. "Well, technically, Collin did it for me since my phone is a loss. He's going to bring me a new one tomorrow. Perks of having a twin."

His lightheartedness falls flat. The fear I felt when Collin called hasn't fully ebbed. I roll onto my side and trail the tips of my fingers down his chest, over bandages, and then back up.

Cal's voice is raw as he says, "All I could think about was getting here to you." His voice lowers even more. "I wanted to come to the safety of home."

I squeeze my eyes closed, though it doesn't stop the tears. I rest my forehead against his shoulder, pressing my face into his arm. I should probably say something, but words elude me.

"I'll get over it somehow, I promise, Jenet. I don't want to drown in my thoughts and I don't want to do this to you or Caroline anymore."

"I'll help however I can," I promise. Whatever he needs, I'll be here.

# CHAPTER 18

## CAL

"Can I stay with Cal today?" Caroline asks as she eats her breakfast.

Jenet peeks over at me and I casually shrug my shoulders. I don't mind if she stays. I think it'd be nice actually.

"Sure. I'll check on y'all for lunch and we'll watch a movie after dinner tonight," Jenet answers.

Caroline angles toward me. "Can we go somewhere again?"

"Cal needs to rest for a bit," Jenet cuts in.

"We'll go somewhere soon," I promise. "We'll look up some places and you can pick, so we'll be ready."

That satisfies Caroline. She listens attentively as Jenet explains how well behaved she needs to be today, mostly because I can barely look after her.

Jenet soon leaves the two of us and as we sit on the couch in the living room, I ask Caroline, "What would you like to do today?"

"Can we go to the park?"

"Sorry, kid. I can't drive right now and I don't have a car."

She makes me laugh as she taps a finger against her chin while she thinks. "Will you draw me something?"

"Yeah, of course. There's a gray bag on the floor in your mom's room. Think you can bring that to me?"

"Sure!" She runs off and within a minute or so, she returns, dragging my bag behind her. She unzips it for me and hands me what I need.

"What do you want me to draw?"

She does the tapping thing again. "Can I have a picture of me, you, and Mommy?"

"That might take me a while," I warn.

"That's okay."

Caroline settles in next to me and watches for a bit. At some point, I can tell she's bored, so I ask her what her favorite animal is.

A butterfly.

After making a request for some colored pencils, she watches me draw her a massive blue and black butterfly. There wasn't really any other color to pick considering that's her favorite.

"What happened to your eyepatch?" she asks.

I nearly wince. I have no clue where it is. "I'm waiting on a new one," I lie, knowing I'll be ordering one. "The other one wasn't all that comfortable to wear all the time."

"Did you get me one too?" she asks.

"Of course."

I don't need the eyepatch. I mean, it'll hide part of the ugliness of my eye, but there's the rest of my face. It's not like I need it to help my vision. Yet I can't help but want to entertain Caroline in her quest to make me more like a pirate.

Within a few minutes, I've finished her butterfly and she gushes over it. I return to the picture she initially requested while she dashes off to her room to store it for safe keeping. She returns and plays with some toys.

The day goes smoothly with Jenet stopping by to bring us

lunch. At some point, I've apparently bored Caroline to pieces.

"Can we paint our nails?" she asks.

I blink at her. She wants to paint my nails? ...No? Plus, my one good eyelid can barely stay open. I'm exhausted and sore as shit.

"I tell you what," I start. "If you promise not to make a mess, you can paint my hands and feet as long as I can close my eyes while you do it." She nods eagerly. "And you have to wake me up when the short arrow on that clock over there points at four. Do you know which one is four?"

She points at it and I nod.

"Okay, do you need help getting the stuff?"

"I got it!"

Off she runs again. I relax as much as I can. Caroline sets her things up on the coffee table. This is probably a bad idea, but I need some sleep.

"Remember, no messes and wake me when the short hand hits the four. Promise?"

"Promise." She holds out her pinky, which I of course link with mine.

Caroline then kneels on the floor, grabs my hand, and I'm out before she even finishes my first hand.

Some time later, the sound of crying wakes me up.

Caroline furiously scrubs at the coffee table now covered with blue nail polish with a towel.

"Caroline?"

She squeaks at realizing I'm awake. "I'm sorry! I was being really careful, I was!"

"It's okay. Mistakes happen. We'll clean it up."

"But I broke my promise! Daddy said you're not supposed to break promises!"

My heart, already in pieces, shatters some more. "Come here." I pat the spot next to me and she drags her feet until she plops down next to me. "Did you mean to spill it?"

"No."

"Then it was an accident and you didn't break your promise. It's okay."

"You're not mad?" she asks, braving a look at me.

"No." I glance at the table. She must've grabbed the towel too late because it's all smeared and dry. "We might need your mom's help on getting it off, though."

"Will she be mad?"

That's a good question. "Not at you," I reply confidently.

"Or you," we hear from behind us.

Caroline swivels, but Jenet saves me from having to do so as she walks around the couch. She props her hands on her hips and smiles at us.

"You let her paint your nails?"

I glance down to see that while Caroline may have spilled the bottle, she managed to finish my hands and feet.

"Sorry, Mommy," Caroline says when I fail to find any words.

"It's okay, honey. Why don't you put your things away while I clean this up?" Caroline does as asked and then Jenet raises an eyebrow at me. "Sleeping on the job as well?"

"She was really good, but I don't think I was physically ready." I rub the back of my neck. "I, ah, have a therapy appointment tomorrow."

"Do you need me to take you?"

I shake my head. I'm throwing Collin a bone instead. "My brother is."

Jenet gives me another smile. She leaves and returns a moment later, rubbing something on the table. She easily cleans up the mess. The rest of the night is relaxing between dinner, the movie, and working on the picture Caroline requested. It's such an honor to have her ask for a picture that includes me as well. The pressure not to fuck up only increases.

Once again, high expectations rest on my shoulders, the weight unbearable since I'll never be able to meet them.

For Jenet and Caroline, I'll try like hell, though.

———

Collin and I don't talk on the drive to my appointment or while we sit in the waiting room. It's unusual, but I don't look a gift horse in the mouth. My name is called and with a sigh, I hobble to the back.

Brenda, a middle-aged woman, sits at a desk and I take a seat across from her.

"It's been a little bit since I've seen you. How are things going?"

"As shitty as can be expected considering I lost my livelihood, further injured myself in a self-induced drunken haze, and now have to deal with the legal ramifications from that. I hate coming here and find it useless, yet here I am."

She ignores my snark. "There's no bright spots in your life right now? None at all? Things with Jenet in the dumps as well?" The skepticism in her tone makes me want to claw out my one good eye.

"Things with Jenet are fine; I've been staying with her since the car accident."

"Still having issues in regard to her daughter?"

I shift in my seat and roll my eye. "Is that really the most pressing matter?"

"You tell me." When I'm silent, she asks, "Why are you here if you find it useless?"

Her question makes me pause. "Because my car accident may not have been an accident and I promised Jenet I'd find a way to move on."

Brenda presses me more on the car accident with that admission. It's pointless because I don't remember what happened. I know with my state of mind at the time what's likely, but I won't ever admit that. She asks me if I feel more hopeful about the future and I'm surprised to find that I do.

Granted, things are shit with my dad and I have no professional career, but that weekend at the beach? If that could be my entire life, I honestly think I'd be okay. The thing is, it can't be my life. Not knowing what I'll do with my life still freaks me the hell out and worries me. And like I said, I made a promise to Jenet.

So, I endure forty-five minutes of hell that feel entirely pointless. How Collin does this on a regular basis, I don't know. Relief floods through me when the session is over. If only I can get back to Jenet's and shut the rest of the world out again.

"Why didn't you tell me about Dad?" Collin asks, finally breaking the silence when he parks in Jenet's driveway.

Fuck. Jenet must've told him about what happened.

"What's to tell?"

"Cal, he's been controlling you since we were kids and you didn't think you should share that with me?"

"What would it've changed?" I ask seriously.

"You could've leaned on me!" he bursts. "Or did you not think I was capable either?"

I roll my eye. "Don't feed me that bullshit, Collin. You had enough on your plate. I didn't want to burden you."

"Oh, like I burdened you?" He doesn't give me a chance to deny that before he erupts with, "You almost *died* because of what he said to you, Cal! God, you can't keep ignoring your issues."

Annoyed, I open the door and slowly manage to get out. Collin sighs, but doesn't interfere. He simply follows suit.

"Dad wants to talk to you before he heads home. He says he feels bad about what happened."

I snort. "Yeah, well, fuck him. I'm not talking to him." I hobble to Jenet's front porch and slowly up the steps.

"Cal, at least let him apologize."

Jesus, even after everything he's learned, he still wants me to speak to our father? The fury that seems to remain on standby lately surges forward as I shuffle and turn.

"For fuck's sake, Collin. No! You only know a piece of what's happened between me and him. Not the full story and if you did, you sure as hell wouldn't be trying to patch things up."

Collin stares at me for a moment. "I'm not defending him or on his side. I just thought it may be easier to move forward if you confront him."

"I'm not interested," I snap.

He's quiet for a beat and then, "What don't I know, Cal?"

A heavy sigh escapes me and I decide fuck it. "The thing with Julie." Collin nods. "Dad knew." His eyes widen. "I called him right after because I knew I overreacted and should go over to see her. He convinced me to stick with my gut reaction. When he found out about you two, you know what he said? *See, son, I told you that it was the right decision. Imagine if she had the kid. His uncle would be his new stepdad.* I ended up telling him it was a false alarm, but still."

Unsurprisingly, Collin is speechless. I hate that he's seeing Dad in a new light, but he doesn't need me to shield him and I don't want to anymore.

"Just leave it alone. I'll reach out to Dad when I'm ready. There are more important things on my plate than my relationship with him."

"I'm sorry. Do you think therapy will help?" he asks as I unlock the door and push it open.

"I don't know. I don't like it, but maybe I'll come around like you did."

"If there's anything I can do—"

"I'll call."

"Will you?" he asks. "At least three times a week?"

I laugh as I ease myself into a seat in Jenet's living room.

"Sure." Three times a week is low for us, but I appreciate that he's not aiming higher.

Collin settles into a seat, taking advantage of being allowed near me again. "How's it going with Jenet? And Caroline? Which one did you let paint your nails?" He smirks and I resist the urge to punch him in the face.

The front door slams open and little feet hammer on the floor as she shouts, "Cal!" She rushes into the room and jumps onto the couch next to me. "Guess what?"

"What?"

She pauses for a solid five seconds before she says, "Chicken butt!" Caroline clutches her stomach and falls sideways with a fit of giggles.

I laugh with her and ask, "Where'd you learn that?"

"Grandpa taught her," Jenet answers as she walks into the room. "Hey, Collin. Are you staying for dinner?"

Collin glances at me. "No, I was just heading out. Maybe some other time." He stands and says, "Oh, I forgot. Brayden wants to know if it's okay to share your address. He wants to stop by to see you."

Gut reaction is no. But Brayden has been there for Collin in ways I haven't and in some weird way, if I allow anyone to see me, it seems like it should be him. I nod in agreement. Collin nods back and waves goodbye to Caroline and Jenet.

"There's a surprise in your room," I tell Caroline, who rushes off before I finish speaking.

"How was today?" Jenet asks once Caroline is out of earshot, taking a seat next to me.

"Fine."

She raises an eyebrow at me.

"Jenet, what do you want me to say?" I ask, simply wanting to understand what she wants me to share.

"How are you feeling? How was therapy? What's going on with your dad?"

"Feeling like I'm jobless. Therapy sucks balls. Collin is telling Dad to kick rocks for me."

She sighs, exasperated with me. She rests her head on my shoulder. "Cal—"

"I'm better today than yesterday," I interrupt.

Her head pops up and she gives me the most gorgeous smile. "Good."

"Mommy, look!" Caroline skids back into the room and waves the new drawing. It's the three of us sitting on the front porch steps. "Thank you, Cal," she says as she climbs onto Jenet's lap.

"Welcome, kid."

Sitting here now, I can't believe I thought the worst thing would be becoming a dad. Clearly, I was wrong because the worst thing was losing hockey. Maybe, though…maybe there is a light at the end of the tunnel.

# CHAPTER 19
## JENET

t's been two weeks of Cal staying with us. It's gone smoother than I'd imagine. He's set himself up a little place in my guest bedroom to do his art. The problem with that is he gets lost in what he's doing. He can spend hours upon hours in there. I've caught him a few times just staring at a blank canvas. That's when he worries me the most.

He goes to therapy once a week. Other than that and being in the guest room, he doesn't do much. We have to drag him out of the house sometimes because he wouldn't otherwise leave. I think he still dislikes the scarring on his face as much as losing his career. He's even been working with a lawyer to handle the ticket he received from drunk driving and still, he handles that on the phone as much as possible.

I'm not sure if it helps or not that he's gotten an update on the guys who ruined his career. Cameras from the parking lot apparently captured the entire thing. Between that and some traffic cameras, they were able to track down all the culprits and charge them with a handful of charges. They weren't even fans who attended the game. The camera footage showed them slipping in during the game and remaining in the parking lot until they jumped him. The reasons why is still unknown as none of them are talking.

Cal still seems lost and I'm at a loss on how to assist. Then again, there are some things he does that reflects he's moving forward.

There is one thing he does that warms my heart a ridiculous amount. He's been drawing various butterflies of varying sizes for Caroline, leaving them in places for her to find. It tickles her so much each time she finds one.

We're preparing to go to the zoo today. Caroline is anxious to go out and do something again. The zoo wasn't my first pick since there will be lots of walking, but Cal insisted he'd manage.

A brief knock on the door has me walking that way. I open it to find a small package on the doormat. Cal's name is written on the front.

"Cal? You have a package," I call out as I return to the living room.

Saturday mornings are for cartoons, so he and Caroline are parked on the couch. I hand him the package as I take a seat next to him.

"Oh good. I've been waiting on this." He rips it open and says, "Look what came, kid." He pulls out something and removes the wrapping to reveal a navy blue eyepatch. "Can't be a pirate without one, right?"

"Right!" she chirps. When Cal pulls out another one, he hands it to her.

"For you, in case you ever want to be a pirate with me."

"Thanks!" She rips it out and I watch as they both put on their respective eyepatches.

I don't know how to deal with this version of Cal. Don't get me wrong; I absolutely love it. But this Cal completely contradicts the one I usually see. He doesn't mind her pointing out anything. He doesn't mind indulging her, like now with the eyepatch he doesn't even need.

Normal Cal still doesn't want to talk much about his old life, as he calls it. He's still worried over what he'll do next. He doesn't want his injury or lack of a career mentioned at all.

Caroline's Cal will let a six-year-old touch his face, question him about his scars, mention ice skating, and convince him to wear an eyepatch like a pirate. He listens as she talks her head off the entire trip to the zoo. He indulges her when he wants everyone else to go to hell and leave him alone.

I love him even more for it.

Moving around the zoo is slow going with Cal's injuries, but neither of us mind. Caroline soaks in all the animals and seems to be mindful of the fact that Cal can't move but so fast. Being away from Raleigh makes a weight lift from Cal's shoulders. Does he realize it? He's smiled more today than I've seen since our trip to the beach. Maybe part of his healing process means he needs to move away.

As much as I hate to think that, if it's best for him and will allow him to move on? I'll fully support him. I watch Cal interact with my daughter. It warms my heart. There must be something I can do to help him heal.

In my humble opinion, his art is his path forward. I'm not sure how likely Cal is to entertain that option after his father tore him a new one. At the same time, I also worry his art doesn't help him as much as I think it will.

"You need something else to do," I can't help but say later that night once we're in bed. Cal grew increasingly antsy as the day wound down and we returned home. "This is downtime you aren't used to. Does the activity that shall not be named help?"

"Some," he admits.

"Have you thought any more about maybe making a job out of that?"

His body tenses reactively.

"Just think about it," I say, not wanting to upset him. Something is on his mind, though. I'm just not sure what.

Cal nods and then almost hesitantly asks, "If I were to attend a wedding in a few weeks, would you go with me?"

"Sure," I answer easily, moving to carefully straddle his lap. "Who's getting married?"

His hands find my hips and squeeze once before his fingers begin to tap.

"Someone from the team?" I asks with a bit of hesitation when he doesn't answer right away.

"Yeah," he huffs.

"Of course I will."

"Thank you." The sincerity in his tone makes my stomach flip.

Goose bumps rise as he slowly drags his free hand up until it cups the back of my neck. It's been some time since we've had sex, especially non-angry sex. Cal seems to pause and hesitate for a moment.

I quirk my lips. "We can be naughty. If you want."

At that, he relaxes and laughs before pressing a kiss to my mouth. My fingers instinctively curl against his shirt. With a bit of reluctance, I pull away a bit.

"Are you...are you okay?" He's still healing from the car accident and I don't want to do anything to cause him more pain. And his mood has been a bit off since we came back from the zoo. He didn't take that damn eyepatch off until Caroline went to bed.

Cal rests his forehead against mine.

"I'm here with you, Jenet. Of course, I'm okay."

Something about how genuine he sounds, like he truly is okay for the first time since he lost the use of his one eye, causes me to smile for a brief moment before I crash into him. Cal returns my kiss as if his very life depends on it. No, as if it depends on *me*. It's such a heady feeling.

It's almost as if every touch breathes life back into him.

Getting undressed is a little clunky and awkward, but Cal's mouth barely leaves mine or someplace on my body as I discard us of our clothes.

We need this. The connection. One full of love and not fury. I'm so overwhelmed by the sweet touches from Cal that I nearly weep. I've missed this with him. He's here, but not fully. Not since the attack and certainly not since the accident. He's not whole. This is the closest I've felt that he's whole again since everything fell apart.

I'll do anything to hold onto this. To hold onto him.

Later, I rest my head on his shoulder and I'm nearly asleep when there's a knock on the door. I bolt upright.

"Mommy?"

"Oh my god," I whisper. I jump out of bed and frantically put clothes on. I throw Cal's at him before rushing to help him for the sake of speed.

Caroline's knocks become incessant. I hurry over to unlock and open the door.

"Honey, what's wrong?"

"I don't feel good. Can I sleep with you?"

I freeze again, but Caroline doesn't seem to notice. While Cal has been staying with us, Caroline hasn't actually ever seen him in my bed or leaving my room in the morning. I'm sure she assumes he sleeps in here with me, but it's not something I've overly addressed figuring less was more.

Caroline walks past me, perks up slightly at seeing Cal, but then stops. Her mouth opens but before she can speak, she leans over and throws up.

I rush to her side and pull her hair back. Caroline whines for a moment after she's done. She walks over to the bed and lifts her arms. Somehow, Cal manages to pick her up. I watch in amazement for a moment as she climbs onto his lap and buries her face in his chest.

Cal rubs her back and I busy myself with cleaning up the vomit before it makes me vomit.

I'm nearly finished when Cal asks in a panicked tone, "Jenet, she's burning up. Should we go to the hospital?"

For some reason, his concern makes me smile. That only makes him frown. I find a thermometer to check her temperature. She definitely has a fever. I grab some medicine for her.

"Jenet?" Cal presses.

"No need for a hospital visit. We'll give her some meds and see if that helps."

"You're the expert," he mutters, causing me to laugh. He shifts a now sleeping Caroline to the middle of the bed and gets up. "I'll crash in the guest room."

I frown. "Why? We've crashed in your bed before."

"That was your only option," he points out. He rubs the back of his neck. "You want me to stay?"

I crawl into the spot he just vacated, move Caroline over a bit more, and then hold my hand out for him. He crawls back into bed and settles behind me.

"You sure she'll be okay? Do we need to stay awake and watch her?"

"She'll be fine," I reassure. "We'll keep an eye on her temp, keep her hydrated, and let her rest."

He takes a peek at her before settling in. I snuggle against his side and quickly fall asleep.

When I awake in the morning, I lift my head and am greeted by a soft smile from Cal.

"Her fever broke at some point, but it's back."

"Did you sleep at all?" I ask.

He shakes his head. "I know you're the expert—and I trust you, I swear—but that didn't help me fall asleep."

I give him a quick kiss and crawl over him to get up. "Get some rest."

Instead of doing that, Cal sits up. "Actually, Collin will be here in a few minutes to drive me to the store. She needs soup and ginger ale, right? We don't have any."

"I'm sure that would help, but you don't have to go."

Cal grabs my hips and moves me back to sit on the bed. "I can't sit here any more. I don't like this." He waves toward Caroline as he stands. "This bothers me a lot. I don't really know what to do with that or how to process, so I need to go do something and she needs soup."

It's then that I notice he's dressed. He must've gotten up at some point to get ready. Cal grabs his crutch and begins to leave the room. I follow because his tone conveys his anxiety and I can't quite pinpoint how much I should be concerned by his comments.

"Cal, wait a second."

He turns to face me just as a knock sounds at the door. "My life has completely turned on its head, Jenet. I never thought I'd lose the game like that. I never thought I'd have a kid, much less a…a…a Caroline *and* I love the kid," he admits as if it's just now occurring to him, though he's said it before. A faraway, surprised look appears on his face before he snaps out of it to continue. "I've fucked up countless times in my life; I don't want to fuck up with her. Or with you. I'm not worthy to be here; it's just a matter of time before I do even more damage than I already have.

"Her being sick? I feel fucking nauseated just thinking about it." He shakes his head as another knock raps against the door. "I just need to run to the store with my brother, clear my head, and I'll be back."

He closes the short distance between us, presses a quick, hard kiss to my mouth, and then heads for the door.

"Cal," I start just as his hand grabs the knob. He chances a glance over his shoulder at me. "For what it's worth, I'm not worried. At all. And we love you too."

A smile breaks out and the tightness that gathered in my chest disperses as he disappears out the door.

# CHAPTER 20
## CAL

Caroline got some sort of stomach bug and was feeling back to herself within forty-eight hours. The heavy, uneasy feeling that started once she was asleep hasn't left me despite her getting better.

On top of that, it's now been a week since my casts came off. For all intents and purposes, I'm healed. I've been getting increasingly more antsy. Will Jenet ask me to leave? Am I overstaying my welcome? Should I be the one to mention returning to my apartment? It's not like I've moved in. I still have my apartments.

Not to mention, it's fucking August. You know what comes after August? September and preseason. I've been doing fairly well, but knowing the season is practically right around the corner? I've been struggling not to fall apart all over again.

"Cal?"

With a sigh, I set the paintbrush down and turn to face Jenet. "Yeah?"

"Someone is here to see you. Brayden?"

No wonder Jenet sounded nervous. Collin asked if he could pass along my address quite a while ago, but I never heard from him. Now that I think about it, if he tried to reach out, he wouldn't have been successful. I blocked every contact in my phone related to the team.

Warily, I follow Jenet out to see Caroline talking Brayden's ear off.

"Hey," he says the moment he notices me. "Want to take a ride?"

Not particularly, but I nod anyway. Jenet lifts onto her toes and gives me a kiss on the cheek. "See you later," she replies softly.

I squeeze her hand in reassurance before following Brayden out.

"What are we doing?" I ask the moment we get into his vehicle, suddenly annoyed that Brayden showed up out of the blue and demanded I go somewhere with him without disclosing where or why.

"You'll see."

He's quiet until we pull into the driveway of a home that looks like it should be condemned. He gets out, grabs two sledgehammers from the back, and I follow suit. Brayden stands in front of the house and then turns to face me.

"You don't know, do you?"

"Know what?"

He hesitates, which is a weird fucking thing to see Brayden do, and then he says, "I'm retired. Announced soon after the season ended. Scotty did too."

My eyes widen and I take a step back as if I just got sucker punched. Why in the hell would they do that?

Brayden forges on. "The concussions. They've left me with headaches and I've really struggled to play the last few seasons. There were a few times when I thought they were going to pull me." He shrugs. "I was like you. Gave the game all I had and now?" He shakes his head. "My health matters more and Deanna is pregnant. I'm retiring to marry my woman and to spend more time with my family without worrying about being gone all the time or if the next hit is going to do even more damage.

"Our situations are not the same, I know that. I got to choose and it's something I wish you had the chance to do too. But it only makes it a little easier. I'm still over here wondering what I'm going to do with all this free time. How much I'm going to miss it. If I'm going to regret it. But this is the best decision for me and my family."

"What's your fucking point?" I interrupt. I'm annoyed and uneasy and I plain don't want to be here. Not playing isn't the best decision for me like it is for him.

"Collin mentioned his concern that you're regressing and still not moving on." Of fucking course. "Just because you're not on the team anymore doesn't mean you have to push us away. I didn't want to show up unannounced, but you have me and everyone else blocked. We're here for you, Cal."

I roll my eye. "What does any of that have to do with being here?" I motion to the house.

"In my spare time, I buy houses, flip them, and then sell or rent them. This is going to be my new job. It's a slower pace, but gives me freedom to do what I want. If you want, you can join me. Permanently or until you figure out what you want to do."

"I don't know shit about any of this and in case you forgot, I got one good eye."

"And it still fucking works, doesn't it?" he snaps back. "Here." He hands me a sledgehammer. As he walks toward the house, he calls out over his shoulder, "Today is demo day. Bringing this girl down to her studs. You can help. Maybe it'll make your ass less cranky."

He's kidding, right? There's no way this would work even if I wanted it. After a moment, I start hearing sounds of destruction. With a sigh, I carefully walk inside to find Brayden in what was once a kitchen, tearing down cabinets that are barely hanging on.

He's an asshole. He always has been and then to drag me out here? What a fucker. He wants me to break shit, I can do that. With a roar, I lift the sledgehammer and begin swinging at the wall.

All the anger over my current nonexistent career that has ebbed and flowed the past few months rises to the surface in full force. I swing and swing until the space in front of me crumbles. Then, I move on and do the same to the next section.

Why couldn't my life continue on as it was? What did I do to deserve this? Then again, I know what I did. I listened to my stupid fucking father. I didn't make big decisions on my own. I didn't listen to my gut. I've lost out on so much because of that.

Then, Jenet came into my life. Things were great. Even as uneasy as I've been about Caroline, I would never want to walk away from them. I still worry I'll fuck something up, but the fact that Jenet has faith in me? That's huge. If only I could stop living in fear.

It seems like hours later before I toss the sledgehammer down. My clothes are soaked with sweat. My body is sore considering this is the most active I've been since May. I swipe my forearm across my face and then look around. As I turn, I spot Brayden leaning against the door frame of the room.

"You did a bit more damage than I would've liked, but I didn't want to interrupt your flow. Feel better?"

"Yeah," I answer honestly. "Call me for demos." Brayden nods. "You have any more wisdom you want to impart on me or can I go home now?"

"Losing the game isn't actually the end of the world. You've got a girlfriend and that kid to more than make up for it until you find the next thing to do. Keep moving forward, Cal, and lean on the people who want to help. And you better fucking show up to my wedding next weekend."

I nod and finally, we're leaving. I text Jenet and ask two things of her. I also text Collin. Brayden is right. As hard as it may be, compared to dwelling on the past, moving forward is my only option and I haven't been doing enough of that.

Once back home, I shower quick and then usher my girls outside.

"Where are we going?" Jenet asks as she starts the car. I still haven't replaced my car and I probably should soon.

"Kid, you wanna go skating today?"

They both gasp. "Really?" Caroline squeals.

"Really. Drive, Jenet," I add since she's staring at me.

"What happened with Brayden?" she asks as she shifts into reverse.

"Nothing much."

I can feel her teeming with the urge to ask all the questions. She'll have to wait. My nerves are too fried to entertain her. I'm basically about to be back in the belly of the beast. And with the plan I have? Yeah, I'm ready to throw up.

I try to clear my mind during the drive and then as we enter the facility. My hands tremble as I help Caroline into some skates.

"Cal, we don't have to do this today," Jenet tells me softly.

There will be no good time to do this.

"Hey, Cal," Collin says as he walks up with Julie and Wyatt. "Thanks for calling. Here are your skates."

I grab them, take a seat next to Caroline, and toe out of my shoes. *Just don't think about it. Just don't think about it. Let your muscles take over.*

"Cal?" Jenet questions.

I ignore her and lace up. Once finished, I stand and hold my hand out for Caroline. She grabs it tightly and we slowly make our way onto the ice. I pretend I'm not even in skates and focus slowly on helping her, instructing her.

My brother and Wyatt join us. It's all painfully normal and nice.

"Cal, can I take lessons and wear pretty outfits like that girl we saw last time?" Caroline asks.

"We have to ask your mom."

"If she says no, will you try to change her mind?"

I laugh. "Sure, kid. I'll do my best."

We skate around for a bit before Collin convinces Caroline to skate with him. He nods at me and I instantly understand. He wants me to skate alone. I expel a breath before pushing off. Part of me wants to take off at full speed, but I've literally got a blind spot and we're not the only ones on the ice.

I skate and skate and I don't combust. My muscles, which have been tense all this time, actually relax. The ability to breathe gets easier. Was this part of what I needed all this time? Is this what moving on feels like?

As I slow to a stop near where Jenet and Julie sit, I lean against the boards. "Hey, get some skates, Jenet." When she stares at me for a moment too long, I add, "And pick your jaw up off the floor."

Julie's laughter snaps Jenet out of it. She throws a smile my way and I wait for her until she steps onto the ice. I take her hand and help keep her steady.

"Caroline wants lessons."

Jenet half laughs, half sighs. "Of course she does." She glances over at me. "You're really okay."

I chuckle. "I'm fine. Is Carol willing to let her spend the night?"

"Yeah. You have something else planned? Where is my boyfriend and what did you do with him?"

"I came back," I reply simply.

"Cal!"

I swivel and grin.

"About fucking time! Come here."

I pull Jenet along until I'm face to face with the person shouting across the ice at me. Zane hooks an arm around my neck and pulls me in for a hug.

"It's good to see you. Hope you don't mind that Collin let me know you'd be here."

"Not at all. Hey, Violet. Hey, JT." JT hides behind Violet, but waves. "Jenet, this is Zane and his family."

Hellos are exchanged before Zane and his son put on skates. We find our way back to Caroline and soon, all of us are skating around. Jenet and Caroline both throw smiles my way. Have they been smiling like that at me? I don't think so. It's like the dark cloud that's been following me around darkened their lives too. The sun is finally coming out again, peeking through the clouds.

After an hour or so at the rink, I say goodbye to everyone and we drop Caroline off at her grandparents'. Once that is done, Jenet and I find ourselves back at home with some takeout. I wanted to take her out for dinner, but being at the rink, while overall positive, has drained me a bit.

"What happened with Brayden?" she asks.

I laugh because I know she's been dying to hear this all day. "He told me he retired and took me to his old house he's remodeling. I destroyed a bunch of shit and felt better afterward. He reminded me I needed to keep moving forward. Trying really hard to actually do that."

She leans over and kisses me. "You seem lighter."

I feel it. I swallow hard and bring up what's been on my mind lately. "I am," I acknowledge. "But, ah, since I'm injury-free, should I plan on returning to my apartment?"

Jenet stabs her chopsticks into her noodles. "Do you want to go back?"

Not even a little fucking bit. Not only because I feel like I'd spiral and have a harder time focusing on the future, but because I love being here with Jenet and Caroline.

Jenet's focus seems to have shifted to her food and she pokes at it. I find myself doing the same as I answer, "I was actually wondering if you'd be open to finding a bigger space."

Her head shoots up. "Really? Wait, why bigger?"

I take my takeout and then hers, closing them and placing both back in the bag. "Let me show you something."

Jenet stands, I find her keys, and then I have her drive me to my old apartments. There's a nervous energy about her, but it's for naught. Instead of coming into my apartment, I enter my studio apartment. Jenet thinks I spend all day in her guest room, painting or drawing, but I actually call a ride to bring me over here.

Dozens of paintings are scattered about.

"What are we doing here, Cal?" Jenet asks as she looks around at all the new paintings. "You've been here lately," she adds.

"Yeah. During the day."

She throws a surprised look my way at my confirmation. And maybe a touch of hurt that I didn't share this.

"I, ah, have been seeing if I can turn this into a business." I wave my hand at the paintings. "A little bit anonymously, I admit, but I've actually been selling them online."

The fact that I've already sold over fifty pieces has been surprising. I share with Jenet that I've been selling them online and all I've learned during that process. I also explain that I want a bigger house for us, so I can have a place to work.

The moment it clicks with Jenet that I want to officially live with her, she throws her arms around me. Her legs lift to wrap around my waist. She kisses me as if we haven't been together physically for years and are just now reuniting.

"Take me next door, please."

I've yet to say no to her and I don't plan on starting now.

# CHAPTER 21

## JENET

"If anyone should be nervous, it's me," Cal whispers.

I can't stop fidgeting in my seat at this utterly gorgeous wedding. It seems like all of the Carolina Rebels are here based on how many people spoke to Cal as we walked inside. That's not what's making me nervous, though. It's what happened before we left the house.

"Relax." He leans over and presses a hot kiss to my neck. "What's wrong?"

"Nothing."

He gives me a look, silently calling me out for being a liar. "Jenet."

The music starts and we all stand, turning to look for the bride.

Cal grabs my hips, pulls me flush against his front, and repeats, "Jenet."

I sigh, turn to face him, and lift onto my toes. "I'm pregnant," I whisper.

I hear a sharp intake of air. His hands squeeze my hips hard just once. His gaze pierces mine, seemingly searching for something. His hands suddenly grasp my face and he leans into kiss me.

Thank god he's holding onto me. The love and passion in his kiss makes me weak in the knees and I nearly sag to the floor, if not for his hold on me. It kills me how he can make a kiss so intimate and swoon worthy with just a handful of swipes of his lips and tongue against mine. A blaze burns within my body, eager to swallow us whole.

Someone clears their throat, snapping me out of the bliss that is Cal. He pulls away and it's then I realize everyone has returned to sitting, except us. Cal doesn't seem to notice.

"I won't let you down," he whispers.

"I know."

"If you two are done, I'd like to get married," Brayden's voice booms throughout the room. Laughter filters around us.

Cal laughs as we finally sit. "You may continue," he calls back, eliciting some more laughter.

I wasn't worried too much about his reaction. While we're moving in a direction I sure love, we haven't talked about this at all. Hitting him with this when we're finally on an upward swing is what made me nervous. Unnecessarily, it seems.

Once the ceremony completes, we move into the reception area. Our table has Collin, Julie, Zane, and Violet. Zane and Violet seem to be checking in with their babysitter while I eavesdrop on Cal and Collin's conversation.

"Ready for the season?" I hear Cal ask his brother.

I'm surprised he's brought it up, but it's like whatever happened with Brayden unlocked something for him. He doesn't even dread therapy anymore and says it's helpful. He went and bought a new car this week, though he's yet to drive it. His lawyer got his tickets reduced, so that part is behind him. He's still nervous about driving due to his sight, though. He'll get there.

"Fucking nervous," Collin quietly responds. "Brayden won't be there. You won't be there."

Julie leans over Collin and says to Cal, "Can you please

tell your brother he can play without you? Apparently, your opinion is the only one whose matters."

Collin doesn't even try to placate his wife. Instead, he's watching Cal, waiting for him to say something.

"You know you'll be fine. You've always been fine. It'll just be weird."

"There. Cal agrees. No more hockey talk," Julie declares.

Cal pulls me into his lap. One hand rests on the back of my neck while the other slips beneath my dress, drawing lazy circles on the inside of my thigh. Loud noises erupt across the room.

"That's Marco. He probably excited to see Rams, who was traded two years ago. They were best friends. The other guy sitting down at their table is Scotty, who retired as well. His wife is super fucking nosy." He nods at another table. "EJ and his wife. She used to be his nanny; they just welcomed a baby boy I hear. His best friend is Derek, who married his sister." My eyes widen at that and Cal chuckles. "Not sure where they are, though. That's Serge and his wife. I can't remember her name."

When I glance at him in surprise, he shrugs. "Met her maybe once and she doesn't really hang with the wives all that much." He nods at someone approaching our table. "Ian and his wife, Sydney. You'd probably like her. Her daughter is around Caroline's age, I think. Maybe a little older, not sure."

"You'll miss them," I whisper.

He sighs. "Yeah."

"Hey, Cal. Good to see you," Ian says.

"You too, Bruiser," Cal replies easily. "Ian, Sydney, this is my girlfriend, Jenet."

I wave hello. Everyone has avoided talking about hockey, I've noticed, except that once with Collin. I'm not sure if Cal appreciates that or wishes they would act as normal. Or maybe they always talk a ton about their summers and their families?

The newlyweds are announced a few minutes later. All eyes are on them as they dance. As soon as the dance ends, someone shouts something about Brayden giving them a show, causing a chorus of laughter. Cal explains that apparently, Brayden sang karaoke for Deanna when they first met; the team apparently teased him for it and haven't forgotten about it all these years later.

We eat dinner, Cal never letting me return to my seat. At some point, people start filtering to the dance floor. Cal kisses a path from my neck up to just below my ear.

"Dance with me."

He pushes me up by my hips, takes my hand, and leads me to the dance floor. I loop my arms around his neck as he wraps his around my waist to pull me flush against him.

"Are you excited? Nervous? Upset?"

Right. The news I shared with him. "I was just nervous about how you would feel."

Cal freezes, releasing his hold immediately.

"Not that you would leave," I hurry to add. "But we have so much going on right now. Trying to find a bigger place. Getting you back to a place where you're happy and—"

"Jenet," he interrupts, wrapping his arms around me again. "I am happy. This isn't what I dreamed for my ideal life, sure." I tense until he says, "But it's better. It's what I actually need. You. Caroline. My art."

He still hasn't told anyone about that. As far as anyone knows, he's simply taking time off. Overcoming how he thinks people will look at him will be the next big hurdle as well as feeling worthy of the life he leads with us.

"Giving in to the urge to be with you, despite my stupid reservations, was one of the best things I ever did. You've stood by me as I lost the one thing I valued most, aside from my brother. Whatever surprises come our way, I'll welcome with open arms."

"You're excited?" I ask.

"More nervous than anything," he admits. "But yes, I'm happy."

"You'll be wonderful," I whisper as I rest my head on his shoulder. "You are fantastic with Caroline and she's not even yours."

"Do you want to get married?"

At this, I snap my gaze up to his. Is he sort of asking me to marry him? Cal laughs at whatever expression I wear.

"Not proposing, Jenet. Just wondering if I should start planning."

Even with the baby, I hadn't thought about marriage. Jasper and I ultimately got married because I was pregnant. I don't want to repeat that with Cal, even if things are different for us.

"I'm not expecting it," I reply. "Propose whenever you're ready. If, you know, you want to."

Cal grins, his skin moving the long scars on his face, scrunching his closed eyelid. He's still no less handsome than the day I met him.

He rests his forehead against mine. "I love you."

"I love you despite all your red flags."

Cal laughs and it's the most beautiful sound I've heard in a while. "You'll keep me around then?"

"For as long as you'll stay."

His lips brush against mine. "Better get used to those red flags then because I'm not going anywhere. I used to think hockey was the best thing to ever happen to my life and it was all I was good for, but I'm starting to think you and Caroline and this baby are the best thing to ever happen to me. Surrendering to the need to be with you was the best thing I ever did."

His hands run up my body until he cups my face. "You're too good for me." I open my mouth but he moves his thumbs over my lips. "You are. Even if I wasn't fucked up with all my red flags, you'd still be too good for me. But I promise to do everything in my power not to let you or Caroline or this baby down again."

"Cal, you've never let us down," I speak, causing him to move his thumbs away. He searches my eyes as if trying to determine if I'm being honest.

"Really?" he breathes. "After everything, you'd still say that?"

I nod. "Life isn't always smooth sailing, Cal. You've handled things the best way you could. There is no letting us down or us being disappointed."

"Fucking perfect," he whispers before kissing me again. We still have a long road to go before Cal has moved on in whatever way best suits him, but we're definitely on that path forward. I can't wait to see him thrive as an individual, as my partner, and as a father. We have a fantastic life ahead of us.

# EPILOGUE
## CAL

### THREE YEARS LATER

"Deep breaths, kid. You got this. You're going to be great."

Caroline shakes out her arms and exhales heavily. Jasper's sports-loving daughter ultimately loved gymnastics the most. She's been practicing hard and is about to go perform one of her routines. She normally doesn't get this nervous, though. Not enough to want to speak to anyone prior.

"Is everything okay, Caroline?" I can't help but ask as she shifts her feet.

Her gaze flicks over to where her mom and little brother sit before returning to me.

"Can I call you my dad now that you're marrying Mom?"

I rock back on my feet from where I was crouched down to be eye-level with her. I was not expecting this question. Caroline rushes out the rest of her words before I can open my mouth.

"I know my daddy died." Her eyes well with tears. "Daddy would be my guardian angel still, but you can be my dad here. Then I can call you Dad like Tyler does, right? And I can be your daughter."

Tears spill over her cheeks and I pull her into a hug.

"Kid, I'd love to call you my daughter. Why are you crying?" I wipe away her tears.

"I love you a lot. Like I loved my daddy and like I love Mom and Tyler. He gets to call you Dad and I was just worried you didn't want to be my dad too."

I'm practically her dad already. Her second dad because I've never wanted to diminish Jasper's memory or replace him. We still talk about her dad often to keep her memories of him alive.

"So I can call you Dad now?"

"Of course, kid." I kiss her forehead. "Now go out there and kick some ass."

She giggles at me, nods, and takes a deep breath. I leave her to take my seat next to Jenet.

"Is she okay?" Jenet asks.

"She wants to call me Dad. I told her yes."

Jenet's eyes fill with tears. She leans over and kisses me quickly before we turn our attention to Caroline. I know one thing for sure. I'll never put the kind of pressure on Caroline or Tyler like my dad did me and Collin. This family I've found myself part of is my entire world. I'll do anything to hold onto it and to make them happy.

I almost feel ashamed that it's taken me three years to finally marry Jenet. On the other hand, I've spent every bit of the last three years trying to rebuild my life to something I can be happy with. I've dived head first into selling my artwork online. My brother knows about it. A few of my former teammates I've remained in touch with know, too. I can remember when I told him and I still feel the relief that came with it.

"It's going to be fine," Jenet whispers with a squeeze of my hand as we walk out to the building in the backyard of the new house we're renting.

Collin, Julie, and Wyatt trail behind us. My brother and I have been rebuilding our relationship after everything that happened and all the wedges I placed between us. It's been weird and tough at times. We're trying to find our new normal. He's having another great season so far and I'm still on a rollercoaster. Some days are definitely better than others.

Tonight, I'm sharing my new path with Collin. I've been stressed all damn day. Hell, all week, knowing this was coming. There are two reasons I'm sharing this with him now, though. One, he's been worried about me, thinking I'm just hanging out at home and occasionally venturing out to help Brayden with whatever renovation he's working on. Two, it's been eating at me that as a whole, I truly am doing okay and he doesn't know.

With a deep breath, I enter the code and the garage door opens. Within seconds, the inside is revealed. Some canvases are propped up, some lying flat. There's paintings and drawings scattered everywhere in organized chaos. My and Jenet's favorites hang on the walls.

"Oh wow; these are gorgeous," I hear Julie breathe from behind me.

"Is this what you've been doing, Cal?" Collin asks. Some of the tension leaves me as I hear the wonderment in his tone.

"Yeah. I haven't told anyone and don't plan to. I have an online store and sell them. It's been going well. I just wanted to show you so you'll know I'm okay."

"This is fantastic, Cal," he says. His gaze continues roaming around my space. "I never knew you could do any of this. I'm glad you've found something that makes you happy." As he turns to face me, he frowns. "How long have you been doing this? The painting and the drawing, not the selling part."

"A long time," I answer simply. "Dad put a stop to it, so I kept it hidden."

Collin curses under his breath. He looks around once more before facing me with a grin. "Happy for you." He gives me a quick hug and adds, "And we fully expect you to do something for us to hang at our house."

I laugh. "Sure." This weight of hiding this, even from my twin, has been resting heavily on me for so long that the moment it lifts, I feel as if I need to grab onto the nearby counter so I won't float away. This is what I've needed more than anything it seems.

It feels so surreal that I find myself asking, "You really mean it? You're happy this is my new career even though it's nowhere near the same field as hockey? Not even a touch of disappointment?"

"The only disappointment I feel is toward Dad. If this is what you want and what makes you happy, then I'm fucking thrilled, Cal. You clearly have a talent. I'm honored you shared it with us."

My throat tightens with the overwhelming emotions building within me. It's too much. So, I blurt out, "Since I'm sharing, Jenet's pregnant."

That sets off a whole new round of excitement and thankfully takes the attention away from me.

While the important folks know, I still don't include my name anywhere on my business. I sell various pieces and take on commissioned work. I don't make the kind of money I used to make, but I make a good living and I'm happy.

The only thing I've left behind is my father. I talk to my mother and still see her, but the wounds my father inflicted are deep. Too deep for me to overcome when he still makes comments about how I'm not living up to my potential. He hasn't said it directly to me, but I've overheard him when I happen to talk to my mom or be around Collin when Collin talks to him. It's enough to know he doesn't feel remorseful at all. He can stay in the past where he belongs if that's how he feels.

Jenet and I bought a house after we got engaged. I think I took my time a bit getting married because Jenet was so blasé about it when I asked at Brayden's wedding. I also didn't want to still be battling with losing my career when I asked. It took a lot longer than I thought it would for me to stop with the ups and downs to finally settle into a steady rhythm.

It wasn't until shortly after Tyler was born and the Rebels won the Cup again that I started regressing a bit. Back-to-back champions? It twisted the knife in my heart even deeper. I was there for every game, too. I wanted to be there for my brother since I wasn't my last year. It was harder than I thought it would've been.

On top of that, my father was trying to butt his way back into my life. With a new grandchild and still thinking I don't work, he felt the need to share this opinion with me. Dealing with that and a newborn, I didn't handle things all that well. The stress and regret got to me.

Jenet grabbed me by the face after one particularly rough night with Tyler. I was in my home studio and had been for hours. I wasn't being as helpful nor a true partner that week. She took my face and brought my forehead to hers.

"Cal, I love you with all my heart. But I can't do this by myself."

Tears began to fall down her face and I immediately felt guilt. She was struggling a bit with some postpartum anxiety. That moment right there made me feel as if I had completely abandoned her. I was a selfish asshole.

"Please stop dwelling and thinking about the what ifs," she begged. "I need you in the here and now with me and our family. Are you truly not happy?"

Her eyes searched mine.

"I'm sorry," I immediately apologized. The shit with my dad was fucking with me the most. That was the moment I decided to cut him out of my life completely. My therapy had cut back to once a month, but maybe I needed to go more often again.

"Are you coming back to me?"

"Yeah." I glanced around and realized I was staring at a blank canvas again. "Let's go inside."

I ushered her back into the house, ran her a hot bath, and sent an email to my therapist. That was the last time I let her down. I ended up having a pow-wow with my father that led absolutely nowhere. But it's been for the best. I've been able to move forward.

Tyler is learning how to skate, but only because he saw his cousin skating and wanted to learn too. My father's lasting impression on me is always on the forefront of my mind when it comes to the kids' sports. They do what they want and I'll support them always.

A round of applause brings me back to the present. Caroline just killed her routine. Tyler moves over into my lap. Life is fully moving forward.

Hockey was a huge part of my life, but that chapter is over. I like this new chapter much better and I plan to make the most of it. Jenet, Caroline, and Tyler are the most important part of my life. I let them down once and I don't plan on ever doing it again. They've literally saved me and I owe them my life and more.

Jenet and I will get married next week, tell Caroline she has another sibling on the way, and then go on a much-needed family vacation.

Jenet takes my hand in hers and squeezes. I glance over and smile.

"I love you and your red flags."

I laugh and lean over to kiss her. "I love you too."

The broken pieces of my life have forged together to form a new picture, a new path. I'll hold onto it with everything I have and spend my life making them all happy. It's the least I can do. There's also nothing else that would make me happier.

# ABOUT THE AUTHOR

 Lindsay Paige is the author of multiple romances, most of which are set in the south. She dabbles in young adult, new adult, and sports romances. She also enjoys writing books with characters who deal with anxiety and depression, issues which are close to her heart. Lindsay lives in the southern United States with her husband, daughter, and dog.

If you would like to hear news before anyone else, interact with Lindsay, and have a place to discuss her books with fellow fans, join Lindsay's League on Facebook. Be sure to visit her website for more information: www.lindsay-paige.com

## ALSO BY LINDSAY PAIGE

Heaven and Hell Duet

Carolina Rebels series

Hearts in Carolina series

The Hourglass Duet

Sanity series

*Bracing the Blue Line*

*Nepenthe*

*Without a Doubt*

*Bending Under Pressure*

*You Before Me*

The Penalty Kill Trilogy

Oh Captain, My Captain series

The Ninth Inning series